COMING OF AGE

COLLECTION

ERIC REESE

ISBN: 978-1-925988-60-4

CONTENTS

PART I

HOMEGIRL AIN'T GONNA MAKE IT

For the sisters out there in America!
The struggle is real!

1

The hotel room was dark even though the windows were open, and the blinds pulled aside. The moon was probably somewhere huddled up and covering itself with a cloud blanket, having abandoned her place in the sky. The skies looked like they were turning in for the night, so they can get their own sleep. Outside, on the streets of Boston, horns announced the movement of cars. Their owners were sleepless and the footsteps could be heard, but the sound didn't reach where I was staying.

My name is Gabrielle. If you saw me sprawled on the carpet, with all these papers scattered around me, you'd think I was dead. I was exhausted from the long travel from New York to Boston. The slow rising and falling of my chest and my eyes pointed I was fast asleep. Sleep had come upon me sudden-like, robbing the papers I had in my company and dragging me along into its comfy walls. Coffee was on the table, untouched, now having gone cold from sitting out. I wanted to stay up to do some research, but that's not happening tonight. My suitcase was watching me from the top of the table where I had left it, unpacked.

A movement, unnoticeable at first, then quietly forming into a silhouette stirred just outside the window. My eyes sprang open. For seconds, I was staring into a pair of eyes looking in on me from another building's window, then there was nothing. I tried getting up to investigate, but my legs had something else in mind. They collapsed near the bed while my eyes strayed uneasily to the window where there was nothing. The deception of the eyes, I thought without really thinking. Sleep patted my head and pampered me straight into unconsciousness again.

"Beep, beep, beep..."

I groaned and rolled over. The alarm sound continued and my hand searched for the terrorist that seemed to scream louder, the more frantic my movements became.

"Where..."

"Beep, beep, beep, beep..."

"... are you?"

The alarm would not ceasefire until either I get up or realize I was dreaming. The clock sat on a shelf above the bed. I got myself together and turned it off.

"Damn. It's early."

I fell back into the bed as my long black hair cascaded down the length of my back.

"I'm so beat," I murmured into the bedsheet.

The bed seemed to hear me and sank me further. With great effort, I rolled away from that magnetic comfort and grabbed my watch off the bed desk. It was 7: 15 am.

"Oh shit! I'm gonna be late." I hurried, scrambling out of the bed.

I was scheduled to come in by 8. Can a sister get a good break in my life, sometime? I'm tired, but it is what it is. The Greyhound got into Boston 11 hours ago and had stayed up most of the night trying to find out ways to impress my new employers. This will be my first real job and I'd be damned if I would let it slip away.

Forty-five minutes was such a short time to get ready. If I did not get going, I'd be late and jobless. Quickly, I went to the bathroom, pulled the door shut and had the shower running in no time. The hot water running down my smooth ebony skin did more than wash me. I felt the fatigue leaving me like it was evaporating. I let myself be drawn to the person staring back at me from the bathroom mirror.

Some say I have a nice body. *Never mind that.* My long natural lashes lined up on the sides of a pair of big eyes, which still looked tired albeit the shower. There were the faint rings around my eyes, but they did nothing to fault the perfect combination those big eyes made with my little nose and my perfectly carved full lips. Even the cynic in me had to admit that I was beautiful and that those eyes could melt a lion's heart. I let my eyes travel down the length of my body, my firm perky breasts and the curve of my hips that began with such subtlety at the waist I kept looking at it, trying to figure out how it had become. I snatched my eyes from the mirror before it traveled down my legs to you know where. I knew what was coming next and did not have time. My hands were already past my navel. I pulled them off my body, closing my eyes and breathing in deeply. When I opened them, I sensed eyes still running over my body and glanced into the mirror. My reflection's eyes were slow in returning to match mine.

2

Detective Gibbons of Boston PD let the car engine run idly for a while he searched for his partner among the hustle and bustle of Boston's streets. The fool could have just stayed home and let his partner come to carry him, but he was afraid he would meet his girlfriend. *Why would someone be afraid of his partner meeting his girlfriend, anyway?* The insecure bastard, Gibbons thought with some fondness. Maybe if he had not teased him so much, he would have met this queen he had heard so much about. No biggy. *Why do his friends think he was always after their girls?* Okay, maybe the detective was too much of a flirt, but that made his job easier. Sometimes all he had to do was get next to the lady, stare at her and information would come tumbling out from the unlikeliest places. *"Just things I do for my country," was Gibbon's motto.* The patriotism he had for America made his views sometimes conflict with his colleagues.

On the other hand, Detective Pete wouldn't share his view with him, of course. He would scrunch up his face to show how disgusting he thought it was, which was very disgusting. Pete was a baby in a man's body and often believed too much, he heard.

Detective Gibbons' stomach grumbled and rumbled. He winced. He had to eat something before the day began facing grotesque picture after grotesque picture of dead people; good, bad, small, big, smart and stupid. He became known for the case of a man trying to take on three armed gangsters single-handedly. Of course, Gibbons quickly became local history but felt a little guilty. He was also stupid, so it was really hypocritical of him calling anyone stupid. He had done stupid things before this, and had scars to remind him of just how stupid he had been in the line of duty.

The passenger door was pulled open and Pete jumped in.

"Hey, bud."

"Hey," Gibbons replied, smiling. Not seeing Pete come up. For a brief second, he wondered what he would have done if it were some hoodlum, thug, gangsta or whatever name he could label a black. *Is that not how it always happening? A career detective who had been a thorn in the flesh of criminals meeting his death at the hands of an insignificant posse member. What if it was one of those criminals pulling the trigger?*

"You okay, Gib?"

"Yeah, man. Just daydreaming"

Damn, Gib's been watching too many movies. He even forgot he hates being called Gib, it sounded like glib. Could Pete not think of something better?

"You don't look good."

"I don't?"

"Breakfast?"

"No," Gibbons replied, "had to wait too long for your lame ass. "

"Too early, Gibbons, too early."

"Early or not, the ass is lame if it is lame."

"Can we get moving?"

"Sire," Gibbons snickered and shifted the gear to drive.

"How's the missus?"

"She's fine."

"Is she as sneaky and dodgy as you?"

"We're a fine match."

"Hmm. Sounds like someone's trying to convince himself."

"You wish."

"Tell you what, Pete. You and your mistress, just you two should come for dinner at my house."

Gibbons saw the now-forming smile on Pete's face.

"Thanks, but no thanks. I'll take a raincheck."

"We live in a fucking democracy, Pete. We haven't asked the lady yet."

"And we're not going to."

"You're saying she has no say?"

"Not in this."

"Bloody chauvinist. "

"Watch the road ahead, remember you're driving."

Gibbons smiled as he maneuvered the squad car through the streets, past early morning pedestrians hurrying to catch the train. The traffic was slowly building up on the main road and some shops that hadn't stayed open through the night had 'open' signs hung at the entrance. Today would be a tough one, Gibbons felt.

"You know, Pete, you can tell me her name. It's not like we can find a woman with that name. Haha."

"Okay."

"So, what is it? Mary? Jane? Brienne? Arya? Anika? Keisha. You look like someone that should be dating someone named Anne."

"Really?"

"Yeah, I know these kinds of things."

"Of course, you do partner. So who were you with last night? Anne? Annabel? Susan? Beth? Sasha..."

"Gwen. I was with Gwen."

"Gee, who would have thought?"

"She's hot, man. I can still feel her mouth on my cock."

"Can you please save me that bullshit this morning?"

"I will but what's her name?"

"Oh gee, we're here. The food dump."

Gibbons found a place to park, then jumped out after Pete. Their clothes fit in perfectly. Gibs didn't feel the usual hairs rising on the back of his neck when he walked through the doorway. Few people paid them attention. It wasn't like they were famous. They hurried their breakfast, so they could get back to work.

As usual, Pete's little eyes were all over the place at once, probing, searching, suspecting. He hated being caught unaware. Yes, Pete did. The first time both of them had ever been caught unaware when he got that nasty scar across his abdomen. He had already asked God to forgive his sins before he realized he wasn't dead.

Pete found them a table at the far left corner where they could watch the entire restaurant. Gibbons ordered a hamburger and a milkshake while Pete had ice cream.

"What the hell? Really man, that's fucking breakfast for you?" Gibbons bursted out.

"I've already had something at home."

"What about a burger?"

"Oh, Touché."

Gibbons bit into his hamburger while his mind wandered away from the restaurant. His eyes looked sad as he pondered on the possibility of leaving his partner and his friend. It was a funny thought, but that was all the thought he had this morning. Gwen from last night was a lie he had made up, so there was nothing to savor from the past day. He would never admit this to Pete, but he stayed up all night thinking about how different things would be if he had a permanent relationship and not just the flings, one-night-stands and romps in Boston's darkest hallways. There was just no one to fill in that empty void in him that he tried covering with the playboy act, the overflowing sexual euphemisms and innuendos. Gibbons was born to live this way or as he thought. Again, he went back to his favorite motto but this time saying it out loud - *things I do for my country.*

"What was that?" asked Pete, eyes narrowed, staring at him.

"What was what?" Gibbons asked as he took a bite of his hamburger.

"Things you do for your country?"

"Oh, I said that out loud?"

Pete looked him again.

"You sure you're okay?"

"I am, Pete. What's this girl turning you into? A fussy hen? I'm okay, grandpa."

Pete said nothing for a few moments as he finished eating his ice cream.

"Well, hurry up, we have to get going."

Pete stood up and went to the men's room. Gibbons watched him go as his teeth sank into the hamburger again.

"Dispatch, 26 Broadway, Boston. A man has been found dead in his office, second floor. Injuries to the neck. The culprit is on the loose."

"Roger that," said Gibbons trying to understand what he said.

"What's this mumble jumble?" sighed Gibbons as he got up to get Pete.

I flagged down a taxi outside of The Owls Hills Hotel where I had stayed for the night. I would be late and that would be a terrible first impression to make.

"50 Broadway Street."

"Aye," the taxi driver replied zooming off.

Could this taxi go any faster? I sat hoping it would. I was a little fidgety and had to get a hold of myself before I reached the new startup company that had hired me. Now, that was where the problem laid; I was finding it difficult to find a worthy job even through I had an Ivy League University degree. Man, I was one of the top students back two years ago, racking up academic awards here and there to the envy of the other students and the admiration of my lecturers. But with all that, I still didn't deem myself worthy of being among the best. Post-graduation realities had caught up with my delicate self-esteem as I messed up interview after interview. I gave the interviewers reasons to send my black ass through the door. There were different doors shut before me, but I rejected the taboo it was because I was black at first, anyway.

Not all of my work histories had been sad songs. I got some part-time jobs in retail where my low self-esteem didn't bother me; leaving me stuttering at the easiest of questions. The random duties frustrated me though. They were not what I had in mind as I walked through the hallways of my alma mater, setting out to be the best I could be.

Now, I was brought here to Boston, Massachusetts for a fresh start. This new company called Revival impressed me. They wanted young talent to expand their brand by doing social media branding and promotional advertising in-person. *Didn't sound hard for 60K a year?* Somehow, I'd kept it together this one time alone, focusing on being the persona I showed everyone back in school. So it is, Boston. I wouldn't feel homesick I believed. The town had the same hustle and bustle that made New York, New York except for one thing; diversity. There were many stories from some of my girls back in NY about the racial epitomes of the city. I told them let me see for myself.

———

My phone rang as the driver culled around a bend, expertly straightening out the steering wheel after he was done making the turn.

"Hello, Ummi. Salam alaikum."

"Wa alaikum as Salam, Gabrielle, did you sleep well?"

"Nope, but I tried. I woke up late."

I whispered the word 'late' like I did not want the cab driver to hear.

"Oh dear, where are you now?"

"In a taxi, on my way to work."

"Did you make your prayers this morning?"

"Come on, mom."

"You should, always, always—" Ummi kept repeating 'always' like it had some sort of enticing quality to her.

"Okay, I will. Gotta go, Ummi, I'm almost at work."

"May Allah protect you."

"Ameen."

I said "Ameen" as a matter of obligation and dutifulness to my mom. Ummi and Abee were devoutly religious. Thankfully, none of their extremities had rubbed off on me and my sister Khadi. I was a think-tank who seldom dealt in sentiments.

"We're here, ma'am."

I was almost sure there was relish in his voice even as I felt my heart palpitate. *"Breath in deeply, girl. You got this."*

I paid the cab driver and got out at a one-story building which had the name of "Revival" engraved on it. *A start-up, eh? Is that what they call it these days to be able to negotiate favorable wages for themselves?* I stood staring at the entrance and envision myself at my desk and before I could see further, a loud honk had woke me out of my daydream.

"Deep breath, deep breath. You're a strong black woman. You can do this," I told myself.

My legs moved slowly and sped up more and more as I got closer to the entrance. My palms were sweaty as I glanced at my watch reading 7:55 AM. I made it in early. Al hamdulilah, perhaps I'm worthy of this blessing. I went inside the building to the receptionist's desk.

"Hello, good morning. Excuse me. I'm supposed to start work today." My thoughts were all over the place.

A blonde receptionist held up her hand and pointed to the phone that she held to her ears. Annoyed, but I masked it with a smile, as usual, while I waited patiently. Time was ticking. The blonde giggled and giggled, clearly wasting time. When she ended the call with '*love you honey*', I realized it wasn't a work call. I checked the time again; the receptionist had taken up 4 minutes of my time chit-chatting with her lover. 7:59 AM.

"Be right back," said the receptionist, smiling. I felt like a fish out of the water.

"Hey, I just want…"

But I was speaking to the back side of the receptionist. I was boiling inside. When I looked in the mirror in the hall, I saw the hurt my cheeks were feeling was because there was a fake smile. I removed the smirk and looked around. People were going to their cubicles or walking around. There were a flight of stairs leading up to the mezzanine. I saw the receptionist going up there. My shoes pinched the sides of my feet, reminding me I had been standing too long. *This white girl deserved to be fired.*

After a few minutes, the receptionist came back.

"Hello, how may I help you?"

You can start by getting rid of your stupid head or pretending it actually works.

"I'm looking for Mr. Brown's office."

"Do you have an appointment?"

"I'm starting today."

"Oh, you're the new girl. You must be Gab…eh,"

the receptionist fucked my name up, blinking with her fake lashes.

"Gabrielle," I completed, almost flinching under the appraisal and hating myself for it.

The white girl has something against me, I was sure. Nothing about her fake attitude was welcoming.

"And you are?"

"Oh, I'm Anne. Listen, go up the stairs, the first door on the right is Mr. Brown's," she said, quickly dismissing me.

It was so abrupt that I stood looking at her, sizing her up. *She doesn't want none of this heat.* This was not a welcome party at all. Anne turned around and was already busy, doing her work. I quickly clambered up the stairs and paused once I got to the door.

"Deep breath, deep breath, deep breath. You're a strong black woman. You got this, sis!" I exhaled.

It was five minutes past 8. That damn white girl Anne made me late.

The door opened just as I raised my hand to knock. The little head of Mr. Brown stared at me from an imposing 6 feet.

"Oh, you," said Mr. Brown

"Gabrielle Muhammad."

"Gabriel. Your folks call females Gabriel?"

"Gabrielle, "I almost choked on what he said.

Brown shrugged, looking at his watch and then over at me.

"Anyway, come in and take a seat. I'll be back in a minute. I need a cup of coffee."

He went around me and disappeared. My mouth was open, and it was hard to close. I couldn't believe his racist ass talking about your folks. I sat down and waited for the tiny man to return. I would have bitten my fingernails if I hadn't got them done on the way up to Boston. The treatment I received so far was appalling. Even though I'm minutes into starting, I worried I had made a mistake and jumped too soon without looking.

"Okay, what do we have here?" Brown's brash voice irked its way down my ears. His lanky frame made him appear like someone who should be singing in an opera as a soprano.

"You're late, I see."

"The receptionist was too busy taking calls when I tried asking where in the building were you."

"Already chit-chatting with the receptionist, hey?"

"No, sir. I—"

"Well, listen, Gabriel..."

"Gabrielle."

"I know how the girls are around here. And believe me; chatting Anna on your very first day isn't something you'd like to be doing if it will make you late."

"I was not chatting with her, sir."

"Yes, we aren't causing global warming either. Anyway"

I wanted to scream. The words were already in my head that read - *Shut up, white boy! You got a loud mouth. Shut up before I shut you up!*

"I...um."

"Listen, Gabrielle, I really like you. I feel you can thrive here from what I see in your resume. So stay focus, ok?"

In the meantime, while he was talking, I wondered if his skin would peel off if he were struck by lightning. Some employees would lose it easily and even go as far as killing their employers.

"Yes, sir."

"Okay, I suppose you'd like to know where you will be stationed.

No, I'm don't, really. When I walked in, I saw 'that place over there is where I would be.'

"Come on and I'll show you," said Mr. Brown getting up and leading the way outside.

On the way to my work area, I noticed so many pairs of eyes looking at me. None were welcoming. They only looking me up and down.

"Good morning," I greeted a white woman who was sitting at the reception at the entrance of my work area.

She acted like she didn't hear me.

"Aw right? I'm going to just keep my mouth shut."

4

Three hours had passed and I couldn't wait for the day to end. There was nothing else that could further worsen the day. I caught my pants' fly open a full hour after going to the ladies' room. The eyes staring at me anytime I got up to get a file or run an office errand made me sick. All of my attempts at starting up any kind of conversation made me look a fool because nobody was interested. I felt silenced from the moment I got in the door. What made things worse was that my pants leg caught onto something underneath my desk and got ripped as I tried to free it.

I was nervous, making errors in my creation of media posts. It was time to regain focus and ignore the BS. Perhaps, I'll survive the first day.

The noon hour had finally hit after the morning

crawled along at an excruciatingly pace. Finally, somebody came up to check on a sister.

"Hey, you're Gabrielle, right?"

I looked up from my cubicle to see a young man in his early thirties, smiling. His hairline was receding but I could still tell he was young.

"Yes," I replied, trying to put on a smile.

"I'm Harold. You came all the way from New York."

Okay, how did white boy know all of that?

"Yep…"

I did not know what to say afterward. Part of me wanted to say 'I'm busy' and end the conversation, while the other was reluctant to lose the first friendly person I had met in this place.

"I guess you can say that."

"Well, see you around. My cubicle is right down there," he said, pointing.

"O—kay!" I thought about how I would get home once my shift ended. With all these people's eyes on me, trying to find a blemish; with my torn pants and jittery body. I would just sit and wait for them to leave, then I would follow.

5

Gibbons had Pete trailing after him as they walked into a murder scene. He had shaken off the thoughts that had been beclouding him on the way and was now focused on the duty at hand. Gibs had to be because their lives depended on that focus which amounted to the difference between life and death.

"What do we have here?" he asked the first officer he met on the scene.

"Detective Gibbons?"

"Yes," Gibs responded holding up his badge. "And this my partner, Peter."

"Okay, I'm Sergeant Daniels. It would appear someone killed the victim with little of a fight, which is kind of baffling."

"How so?" asked Gibbons.

"Well, the table is facing the door. His body is facing the same direction then if you look closely, you'll see a box stacked up by the window," the sergeant explained.

"From where he was sitting, he might have expected someone was coming.The door appears to be left unlocked."

"Perhaps he was sleep when the assailant came in?"

"Yeah, but that's a long shot."

The men walked inside the room, and Gibbons smelled the familiar coppery scent of blood. That scent still was fresh to him after all these years, but not Pete. Pete was new to homicide, only spending six months in division.

The dead man had a pen gripped tightly in his right hand and his head was on top of the files he had been working on before his death. The blood was drying up and gave another shade to the table's dark red vinyl. The flies were already soaked in blood.

"He had cameras in here, didn't he?" asked Gibbons.

"Um, the receptionist downstairs said he always had them off, and yesterday was no different."

"Who's he?" asked Pete.

"Mr. Morgan Brown, son of late business mogul,

Octavius Lucious Brown. He's the owner of the new startup company here called Revival."

"The name Lucious? Who the hell would name their son that? What is he, Greek?"

"Don't know, sir."

"How about the cameras outside the door?"

"We've asked for the footage from the building manager. If you're ready, we can get it when we leave to go back to the station."

"Wait," Pete said, going around the body.

He lifted Brown's head gently and found a knife still stuck in the throat underneath his suit jacket.

"Gloves."

A detective standing by the door handed Pete a pair. Pete put them on and gently slipped out the knife. Then, he examined the neck. There was something that had been carved into the man's neck; something that had taken some precision.

"Black girl lover," Pete whispered.

6

It was 7:00 PM. I had waited for everyone to go home for the night. I buried my head into my desktop like my life depended on it. People were walking past me all day and I forced myself to not look up. It seemed like my co-workers' stares would never end. But finally when everyone seemed to have left, I stood up and grabbed my bag, using it to cover my torn pants. Time to go home and who knows if I'll be coming back.

I hadn't seen Mr. Brown come down to my cubicle since earlier. He probably was up there in his office working. Thinking of him made my cheeks hot as I thought back to the incident earlier in the morning. I wanted to handle my business and get something off my chest. We had to clear something out or at least come to some understanding. I'm not with the word *"folks"* nor did I like the way he character-assassinated me about Anne. As I grabbed the rails and going up the stairs, I felt my temperature rising. I was pissed and wanted to deal with somebody in here. There has to be some accountability. I reached the door of my employer and grabbed the doorknob but couldn't turn in. I stayed on it, meditating.

"Deep breath, deep breath," I exhaled.

I wanted to turn it and bulge inside his little office. We need to set the record straight that Anne had been a huge pain in my ass today and how does he dare to defend her. I'm no chump and I can't just let the man get away with what he allows to go on in this office.

I waited and waited and then coward up. I let go of the door handle. *What exactly was I hoping to achieve? I wondered. I thought I heard frantic movements behind the door, a cough, and then a bump.* I turned away and returned the way I came. Whatever the man was doing in the office was not my business. Maybe he was getting some.

No one was around in Revival's office building. When I got on the elevator, nobody boarded with me. The security guard at the front door sat and just looked at me. *Poor old man!* I didn't even say bye to him as I walked out. The only thing on my mind was finding a cab to take me back to Oak Hills.

"Taxi! Taxi!" I yelled. A driver pulled over and we were heading to the hotel. There was a pub along the way. I told the driver at the driver to let me out there. My body felt cold, like the cold hands of dread were trifling with my intestines. Something's wrong! But a hot drink would remove the coldness.

———

The pub wasn't big and had a lot of neon lights in the front. I expected it to be more people being that it was rush hour. However, in my present state, I'd rather it be empty.

"Rum, please. Without ice."

The bartender came back, and I gulped it down so fast that my throat was burning.

"Another glass, please."

"Are you okay?" asked the bartender as he poured.

"I really don't know."

I drank the second one, slower than the first.

"You must be new here? I haven't seen you around before."

"Is that a problem here?" I was feeling tipsy.

I whipped my hair to get rid of the strands blocking my view.

"No, no. I'm Andre. What's your name, honey?"

"Gabrielle." *How this white boy got a black boy name, I wondered.*

"Gabrielle, your skin is so radiant."

"That's the first line I've heard?"

Andre chuckled watching me for sometime before he asked, "What's on your mind? You look stressed."

"You won't understand."

"Why because I'm white?"

"Oh, you know, then. Pour me another drink."

"One thing you fail to realize," said Andre as he poured. "Is that there's black in all the white and there's white in all the black?"

"Whatever."

"You had a rough day. Most of the customers laugh at my jokes. Let's talk about it?" He looked genuine. *This little white boy is sweet.*

"Nah, I'm good. I don't want to talk about it."

Andre went to serve someone else, starting up a conversation and talking to death. I wished it was that easy for me here. While Andre was busy chatting, it was my signal to bounce up out. It's getting dark, and I had to get back the hotel before the lynch mob shows up.

"Leaving already?" Andre called after me, realizing I was leaving.

I turned around and glanced at the table to make sure I hadn't forgotten to drop any extra bills.

"Come around again. We can talk about whatever."

"I'll see."

———

It took me 15 minutes to get back to the hotel. The bellboy kept looking at me like I was a rare exhibit, and even Billy, the receptionist whose name tag was falling off. They responded nonchalantly to my hello. I got to the first floor and put the keys in the door. The tiredness in my eyes overwhelming me. I need sleep. The key turned smoothly in the lock, clicking the door open. Once I shut it and walked in, I sensed someone behind me inside.

"Welcome, Miss. Gabrielle," Gibbons announced.

"Who.. who the hell are you?"

"Detective Gibbons at your service."

"I don't remember calling the police."

"I'm sure you don't. I'd like to take you in for questioning."

"What's this about? You can't just walk into my room...! Who gave you the key, anyway?!"

"Your employer, Mr. Brown's dead."

"My employer is… what? What did you say?"

"Mr. Brown's dead."

"No, don't play with me! What the hell do you want with me then?"

"We were wondering if you can come with me and my partner, Pete to help us clarify some things."

"Brown's dead… dead?"

"Yes."

"Let me go change and I'll be right out. Oh my God!"

———

During the drive to the police station, I was quiet and rebuffed every attempt Gibbons made to engage with me in a conversation. They escorted me to an empty room with a steel table. I asked was I under arrest. They told me that as of now; we are looking at potential suspects without giving me a direct answer.

"You're the only black employee at Revival, is that right?" asked Gibbons.

I sighed. Why does everything have to be about color? I shifted my gaze over to Gibbons' partner, Pete. His face spelled all the letters of impatience. I don't like him.

"I don't really know. Today was my first day. I was at my cubicle all day."

"Were you discriminated against anytime during your day at work?"

"Yeah, you can say that."

"Is that why you did it?" Pete interrupted. "You were tired of taking those crackers' shit? Weren't you?"

"Hmm. I just started working there. I don't know what you're talking about?

"Well, you thought about it all day how to get back at Mr. Brown. You were tired of those white people looking at you like a piece of shit. Weren't you?" added Pete.

"I don't know what you're talking about, sir."

"You killed Mr. Brown, didn't you? You waited till everyone was gone, then went upstairs to kill him."

"Why would I do that? The man just hired me."

I looked at Gibbons and wanted to know what was going on behind his hooded eyes.

"Everyone we've talked to at Revival felt you didn't deserve the job. You were making errors and in and out of the bathroom all day."

"That's my business. Again, I have no reason to kill Mr. Brown. I only saw the man once today when he took me to my desk."

"Who does this knife belong to then?"

The knife that Pete produced, was thrown on the table in an evidence bag.

"What? I've never seen this knife in my life."

"Well, it has your prints on it," persisted Pete.

I shook my head, not believing a word they were saying. They must have seen the video which showed me sneaking up to Mr. Brown's office. They were trying to pressure me to give a confession. Well, at least Pete was. I don't think the other detective, Gibbons, believed I killed Mr. Brown. He had such kind eyes but looks are deceiving.

"I have not touched that knife in my life," I said. Maybe Gibbons would believe me. He sat quietly, letting Pete, carry on with the interrogation. The man looked like it was of any use. I didn't do it, and I think he knew it.

"Miss. Gabrielle, where were you from 7:15 pm to 7:30 pm this evening."

I thought over and over about where I was being careful to answer. "In the bar, pub, tavern whatever y'all call it here down the street a few blocks away from the company's building. I was talking with a bartender, named Andre the whole time. I think that's his name."

"A black bartender in Boston? You're lying, young lady?" said Pete.

"I know the kid, Pete. He's a white boy with a black name." Gibbons exhaled in relief.

Detective Gibbons suddenly appeared handsome in my eyes. Maybe under different circumstances, we could have see where it would go but not tonight.

"You can go home for now. But don't leave town until we contact you. We may have more questions."

"Yes, sir."

7

———

Back at Oak Hills Hotel, I stared out the window. The streets were empty, and the nightfall shielded the side-walks. I had a heavy heart waiting in anticipation about what will happen next. I couldn't leave town, and Detective Pete kept reminding me that if I did before they called, they can arrest me for obstruction of justice.

I was tired. My eyes followed the cars as they raced each other up the street. My gaze went to the phone near the desk in the room. I needed to talk to Ummi. She was the only one that could calm me down. The phone rang for a long time before someone answered.

"Hello, salaam alaikum."

"Hello, Ummi. It's me, wa alaikum as salaam." I sniffed feeling cold.

"How are you?"

"I'm not good, mom. I'm losing it. The police accused me of murder but they believe my alibi."

"What! "What the hell are you talking about girl? Stop being silly."

"It's true, Ummi. Someone killed my boss."

"When?

"Tonight, they took me in for questioning, but they are checking out my alibi."

"Come back to New York now, Gabrielle. I'll call your father. He's at work."

"I can't yet. The detectives said I can't leave Boston. They also said that my fingerprints were found on the murder weapon. I don't know how."

"Oh, Lord have mercy. Please make dua!"

I heard Ummi talking to a male probably my dad. I wasn't trying to make him upset.

"Mom, I'll call you back."

"Gabrielle, wait. Your sister wants to talk to you."

"I'll call tomorrow. Tell Khadi I miss her. Everything will be okay, I hope."

"*Masalama.*"

I walked to the window again, struggling to control my emotions. I was shaking and was about to cry.

———

Meanwhile, it suddenly hit Detective Gibbons just as he was going late night grocery shopping. There was something he and Pete had overlooked. He knew that Gabrielle was not the murderer but couldn't let her off the hook unless someone else emerged as a suspect. He called Pete once he got home.

"I have something. We need to look at the video footage again."

"What the hell, Gibs. It's 2 AM. I'm sleeping with my babe."

"Meet me at the squad room in thirty minutes and make sure you bring coffee and donuts."

With the grocery shopping completely off Gib's mind, he sped the car towards the station forgetting everything he bought.

Detective Gibbons got back to the precinct in ten minutes and sat in his car into the police's parking lot for a few minutes. Exhaling, he slowly walked through the precinct's doors. There were a few uniformed guys on duty, sipping coffee waiting for calls for the night.

"Hey Bob," Gibbons greeted the eldest officer on the floor.

"Come to join us for night shift?"

"You wish, you cocksucker."

Gibbons walked to the back of the precinct to the video room where he checked out the log and took the footage labeled "Revival Murder." He slotted it into the computer's DVD drive while the officer went up front. He rewound it to the beginning and watched. The camera focused only on the front of the office door. As he were watching, Pete came in and joined him.

"What is this all about, Gibs? Getting me out of the bed of one of my honies."

"Fucking dickhead. Just watch. So far, everyone is entering and leaving Mr. Brown's office throughout the day."

"Is that supposed to be the damn nightly news?"

They sat for nearly twenty minutes while Pete was nearly falling asleep until Gibbons rewound it back a little after spotting something.

"Wake up, Pete. See this guy."

"Yeah?"

The person had a reclining hairline and was smiling.

"He never came out after 6:30 PM."

They re-watched the footage from beginning to end and concluded that the reclining-hairline guy never came out of the office.

"How did the hell did he leave then? We watched the tape all the way until we came," asked Pete.

"The window, perhaps."

"We need to call for the street camera footage. We've got our guy."

———

I stared at the TV with empty eyes. I took me awhile to realize the buzzer was ringing. I didn't know that hotel rooms had them. I hurried. Detective Gibbons was there, looking like a cast out of a movie. It was 5:09 AM.

"Sorry for disturbing you. I had to tell you in person you're free to go."

"I am?"

"Yes, can I come in?"

"Sure." Detective Gibbons stood there, not sure of how to proceed further.

"Wanna a cup of coffee?"

"No, thanks. Just listen up. I won't be long. It turns out that the murderer is a guy name Harold. Do you know him?"

"We've met."

"Did he shake your hands with gloves on?"

"Maybe. I don't know. Hmm, I think so."

"That may explain the fingerprints on the knife. We got them off the gloves he wore."

"Are you sure?"

"I believe so. He went inside Mr. Brown's office when he stepped out for lunch and was there, waiting until everyone went home. The street camera caught him climbing out of Mr. Brown's window around the time of the murder."

"Why the hell would he kill that poor man?"

"Apparently, we found out that Harold was fucking with Mr. Brown's wife and wanted to get rid of him before he found out. Excuse my French. Your arrival was his chance he couldn't afford to miss."

I tried digesting all of this with little success.

"Well, I'll be going now," said Gibbons, walking towards the door.

Deep down inside, I wanted to stop him from leaving and I could tell he didn't want to take off either. If I wasn't Muslim, I'd tell him to come chill with me for the night.

While at the door, Gibbons asked, "Will you still be staying in town?"

"I don't know yet," I replied already knowing since Ummi told me to come back, I'd be on the first thing going to New York in the morning.

"Well, take my card. Maybe we can have some lunch one of these days. You know?"

"Yeah, right? Not today, Gibs. I'm Muslim and I can't just be hanging out with boys like that."

"Oh, I forgot to mention that you may be subpoenaed in court as a witness when we catch Harold for the murder trial. I'm sorry. It's standard procedure."

"Oh my God! Why me?"

Detective Gibbons left smiling, walking through the corridor with a schoolboy swagger like he got one on his way to his squad car.

I started packing, knowing for sure, it was time to go. Hey! I got a good life in my room at Abee and Ummi's house. Sometimes, you have to just reset and thank Allah for another day.

PART II

HOMEGIRL AIN'T GONNA MAKE IT

Everything is very black and white for me. I
don't really like playing mind games.

— Zayn Malik

BACK IN NEW YORK

I hate airports. Crowds cause my anxiety to reach uncharted levels. Don't get me wrong. I enjoy flying, but dealing with so many people and every airport procedure from entering and exiting the plane was a bit of a stretch.

Moving through the crowd, I ignored the stares. My hands were sweaty, causing my grip to loosen. Damn, suitcase almost slipped out of my hand.

I tried getting to the exit as fast as possible. My mom and ad didn't know I'd be coming back home. Sensing the fluctuation of my mood, I took a deep breath. "Taxi," I yelled. I didn't have time for a Lyft.

My mother "Ummi" played the biggest role in my life when dad was away working. She gave me and my sister everything and I am forever grateful. I could only imagine the expressions on their faces, the moment I walk through the door.

A taxi stopped in front of me. An African man got out and grabbed my suitcase and placed it in the trunk. His white teeth was more than his smile as he opened the door for me. His kindness weirded me. "Is this the new New York City?" I wondered.

"Where to Miss?"

"St. Greenwood. Number 13." I barely made eye contact, constantly checking the time on my phone.

New York's a wonderful city. I call myself lucky spending my whole childhood here. Growing up in a lower-middle class family had its trials, but Alhamdulilah (praise be to God), we were blessed.

My phone buzzed, a text message read: *Where are you? Ummi is freaking out.*

My family always made such a big deal out of everything. I thought I told Khadi not to say anything before I came. I decided not to text back and shut off my phone.

Traffic was horrid. It was the second thing I hated the most about New York. I was nervous thinking I'd have to spend way too much money on this taxi. *"Why didn't I just call Lyft?"* Hopefully, the ten-dollar bills in my purse would cover everything. Otherwise, I would be forced to get this driver to take what I had.

"You look like you're not from here. Am I correct?" the driver said looking through the rear-view mirror.

Wrong.

"I'm from here." I looked out the window not paying him any mind. "*What kind of a question was that?*" I thought.

"Oh really, the girls here talk a lot. Many of my —" said the driver turning down one block.

"*I'm not one of those girls,*" I said to myself. The beeping of cars stuck in traffic was bugging me and it looks like we would be here all day.

"Just tired, that's all."

"How was thee flight?"

"*People just don't know how to mind their damn business these days.*" I thought.

As he was about to say something else, my phone cut him off. It was Ummi. I panicked, thinking my tone would give away where I was. I might as well not answer.

"*I'm gonna be home soon.*" I texted.

I wasn't a good liar. The taxi started moving finally after a forty-five-minute traffic jam. I was upset we took so long crossing Manhattan bridge.

"How much time do we have left?"

"Not much, it appears to be clearing up," said the

driver making a swift turn. "We're on the main road now, minutes away."

Leaning on the window, I gazed. It was odd that this part of New York City was in such a calm state. The neighborhood we lived in was known for robberies and drug dealing. Just like many of New York's streets were. I'm just glad I wasn't caught up in the bullshit growing up.

As we got closer, my heart raced. Ummi was the type to never believe what I said. *Would she believe I was such an innocent girl while I was away?* I scratched my head as we reached my street. The garden was still intact. Ummi took care of it on weekend mornings.

"You can drop me off here, sir. Thanks." The driver stopped and was kind enough to get my suitcase out of the trunk. "Here you go!"

"Breathe Gabrielle. You're home." I thought as I approached the steps.

From the outside, it looks like they're remodeling. *Wow!* However, as much as I wanted to stay here, I had to get on with my life.

"Guess who's back?" I yelled out, loud enough for my next-door neighbors to hear. Then, I heard footsteps running to the door.

"Gabbie!" My sister, Khadi, hugged me so tight that I couldn't breathe. "Let me go, girl!"

"You've got fatter," she said slapping me on my back.

"It's been nine weeks what do you expect? Ha-ha." Finally she let me go. "What a little brat!" I thought.

"Where's Ummi?" I put my suitcase next to the door and walked inside.

"Grocery shopping. We need food up in here," said Khadi following me to the living room. I plopped on the couch and looked around. There was a single colorful plant in the corner which matched the color of the living room.

———

We talked about happened in Boston. Khadi was a talker, asking every question possible. It's always been like that and our five-year difference seem to help me show her who's the boss.

"What's up with school?"

Khadi stared at her feet. There was obviously something going on.

"Is there something you're not telling me?"

Khadi never had problems at school as far as I

knew she always made friends and was good with all her teachers.

"We've had a lot of tests lately. That's all." She said playing with her fingers.

"There's something going on. This girl always told me everything, so it was strange she was keeping secrets. Does she have a boyfriend? Nope. Maybe the time I was away left a bad taste in her mouth? Nah. I don't think so." My thoughts were just pouring and pouring

"Bad grades?" I kept pressing, not giving her the chance to get off this one.

"Not really. Enough about me. Did you meet a husband up there?" Her eyes lit up as she was at the end of the couch chiming in. This girl is silly. She was trying to change the subject.

"No time for that. I'm working." I barely had time for anything. Boston was a mess. My boss got killed over his lover, and they tried to set me up for it. "

I wondered when Ummi was coming home. She always took her time shopping, trying to get a cheapest deal in town. I walked to the kitchen, to make me something to eat and noticed that the fridge was damn near full. *"Why did she go grocery shopping then?"* "Hmm," I sighed.

"Hey, you want anything!?"

"Make me a sandwich!"

I rolled my eyes. "Not today? You're grown. Come make it yourself," I shouted while pouring cereal in my favorite bowl.

"Well, you asked me if I wanted anything." Khadi came to the kitchen. I watched her make her sandwich while I ate my cereal.

"Ummi is sure taking her good ole time," I said looking out the window. Maybe Khadi knew something I didn't. "Did she go with Abee?"

"Nah, she went by herself," said Khadi grubbing. "Leave her be. It'll be a miracle if she came back soon. I don't know what's going on with her these days. She's always taking her time."

Hmm. Was there something wrong? She always told me everything. I would be so mad if she was hiding something from me.

"Is everything good with her at work?"

"Yeah, she's good. I guess."

Is Khadi lying or telling the truth? I didn't know what to believe. The girl was mischievous, but didn't lie often. We sat in the kitchen looking at Martin until the front door opened. My mother was holding plastic bags and behind her a man carrying some.

"Gabrielle!" she screamed. I didn't know whether it was because I caught her ass with another man or because I arrived.

"I—I didn't expect you to be here," said Ummi putting the groceries on the countertop and then coming to hug me. The stranger kept staring at us and didn't leave out.

"Ok, you can leave now. Thanks for helping my mom," I said.

He chuckled and Khadi looked at me weirdly.

"Maleek, don't just stand there. Come on in." Ummi smiled, and I was confused.

"Where's Dad?"

No one said anything. *Where's Dad?* I was about to have another anxiety attack..

"Gabrielle? I have something to tell you."

"Oh my God! Don't say—"

"No, child. He didn't die."

"Then, what is it, Ummi?"

"Your father and I divorced before you left and waited until you went to Boston to go our separate ways."

"What? You're so wrong. Damn, Ummi. You couldn't tell me?"

"Gabbie, my love. I was ashamed. We tried to make it work for years but things just didn't work out. I'll always love him and he will always love me. Now, give Maleek salaams." My mother pushed me.

"Salam alaikum." I mumbled, eating my cereal, distraught.

"Wa alaikum as Salam. I'm Maleek, it's nice to finally meet you, Gabrielle." He sat down close. It felt weird and uncomfortable. My sister had a look on her face that made me want to smack the black off her.

"Maleek and I met at work and we're planning to marry soon." Ummi sat down and I almost choked.

"I'm done. Y'all can have your wedding in peace without me." I got up, left my bowl, and stomped upstairs, leaving them in the kitchen.

I laid on my bed thinking about my father. *Where did he go? How could Ummi forget about him so easily?*

There was nothing else for me to do was yell. I stuffed my face in my pillow to block the sound. I supposed coming home was going to be a joyful occasion, but this is hell.

My eyes were fixed on the ceiling, I tried ignoring the emptiness how I felt. There were no positives. I looked at my phone, seeing my friends having fun on WhatsApp. I miss them but I'll give myself a few days of self-care, first.

———

An hour passed since that Maleek thing came in my

house. As I was falling sleep, Ummi came busting in my room with a death stare.

"What is it?" I asked, rubbing my eyes.

"Why were you so rude to Maleek?" Ummi raised her voice for the first time in years.

"What do you mean?" I tried to act as if I didn't know what she was talking about. She had no right coming into my space like this.

"I saw the way you were looking at Maleek, Gabrielle. Can't I be happy for once in my life?"

"Did you even love Dad?" I looked at her dead in the eye.

She stared at the ground and said, "You can't punish me like this. I deserve some peace in my life."

I couldn't believe what she was saying. She acted like Dad never made her happy. I was beyond hurt, so I pulled the comforter over my head. She was still standing there. "Go away," I thought.

"Maleek and I are going out to dinner tomorrow and Khadi's coming with us. I expect you there."

With no reply, I shut my eyes, waiting for her to leave. She did, storming out of the room in a fit and slamming the door. I cried until I fell asleep.

WHO IS MALEEK?

I was never a morning person. The pain from Ummi's love affair didn't leave overnight. I got up to go to the bathroom and almost tripped over the towels, left on the floor. Ummi didn't bother cleaning up, which meant the next person had to do it.

I mostly spent the thirty minutes me spent inside the bathroom, cleaning it and hoped I didn't see Ummi for the rest of the day. After praying, I went downstairs to make breakfast. This day wouldn't be easy if I had to talk to Khadi.

Ummi had left already and Khadi sitting on the couch, playing with her phone. I had the usual; a bowl of Sugar Smacks. The silence would go away once my sister sees me. *Maybe Ummi is out with that guy, Maleek? Who knows?*

"You're up early, never thought I'd see this in my lifetime," joked Khadi.

"I'll smack that grin off your face. Don't even start."

"Don't get mad at me."

I wasn't in no mood for the bullshit and just want to spend my day alone. I rushed back upstairs after eating. Her words hurt me, causing my emotions to be all over the place.

———

About an hour later, a neighbor started playing eighties R&B jams which helped me get motivated to clean up. I hummed along until a knock on my door.

"Yes?" It was Khadi.

"Ummi wants you downstairs."

"Tell her I'm good. I have nothing to talk about," I said, folding my comforter while ignoring her stare.

When did she get back? It must be something about the damn dinner. Khadi came in here dressed like she's going out.

"So, you're going with them?"

"Just come downstairs. Ummi will kill me if you don't."

"No."

Khadi stomped and stood at the door, waiting for

me. I love her so much, but sometimes I wanted to choke her. Damn girl gets on my nerves.

"What do y'all see in that Maleek guy, anyway? He's using Ummi."

"I don't know. Ask Ummi. She's the one who has feelings for him. I'm not getting involved."

"Not getting involved? You're her daughter for God's sake!"

Khadi shushed me, but I didn't care if mom heard me. I was right.

"Give me five minutes."

———

I followed Khadi and the second we got downstairs, Ummi was standing right there. "Are you two ready? We don't want to keep Maleek waiting." She tried pushing Khadi ahead, but I grabbed her hand first.

"You are forcing her into this, aren't you?"

If looks could kill, I would be twenty feet deep right now. Where did I get the courage to stop her? Sure enough, I was lucky enough Ummi didn't smack the crap out of me.

"In fact, Gabrielle I'm not. She wants to go." She took Khadi's other hand and tried pulling her away. I held hers, not giving in.

"Is it true, Khadi?"

"Yeah."

This girl wants me to slap the black off her. Why would she want to go out with them? This is between Ummi and Ma-LEEEK.

"Ok, I see who's about themselves," I said looking at Khadi and Ummi. I was ready to head back to my room when Maleek came to the front door.

"*Salam alaikum.* How are the ladies of the house? Gabrielle, I'm so glad you are coming."

"Not me," I whispered.

"Let's chat in private, if that makes you feel better." As he spoke, I was already walking away.

There will be always be resentment towards Maleek for not being my father. I saw this as the perfect chance to make myself clear about staying away from Ummi. She always made foolish mistakes. I hated to admit, but this was the most obvious.

"Okay, Maleek. I'll be right down." I took out the worst outfit I had. *You think I care?* When I got back downstairs, they were sitting in the living room, looking exhausted.

"Are you finally ready?" said my mom frustrated.

"Yeah."

We went out and Maleek drove his car to the front of the house. *"Damn, we're going in his car?"* I sighed.

It sure wasn't a luxury ride as I kept trying to guess why Ummi was interested in him. Maleek watched us get in the back while he opened the door for Ummi. *This guy is really pointing on a show. How pathetic!*

———

Nobody talked as I kept peeping at Maleek through the front mirror. I couldn't believe I even got myself to go.

"Did you make a reservation?" asked Ummi. They turned a question into a million. Twenty minutes later, we arrived. The restaurant was a simple black-owned family eatery.

There's something up with this Maleek guy. I'm sure. Khadi and I followed behind Ummi and Maleek. I took slower steps on purpose while Khadi was close to Ummi.

"Hurry, Gabrielle!" said Ummi waving her hand and not turning around. I rolled my eyes. *This outing needed to be over quickly. Let me just talk to the man.* Once inside, there were few guests. On a Friday night in New York, this is quite strange.

Maleek lead us to a booth that had nice leather couches. *Okay, but I don't really care.*

"Where's the menu?" said Ummi as she put her handbag down.

I played my phone, not paying attention as they went on talking. Khadi was chiming in which made me pissed. *Should I put a sock in her mouth for the sake of it?*

"So, Gabrielle, what were you doing in Boston?"

"Did someone say something?"

Maleek paused while Ummi looked at me.

"Just was working in an office. I guess you already heard about my ordeal."

"Yeah, so unfortunate. Let's not talk about this tonight. Are you looking at anyone for—?"

I cut Maleek off with the most fake smile. "None. Next." *Why bother me with such questions? I'm not feeling him.*

Ummi and Maleek then turned back to their conversation. The waiter came by and interrupted. "What would you like?" asking me first.

"Caesar salad, with sparkling water." I smiled, feeling sorry because the man looked so tired. He took the rest of our orders and I went back to looking at my phone.

"So, Khadi, how's school going?" Maleek interrupted her Snapchat browsing. I kicked her under the table.

"Good, good. Too much homework but I'm managing."

This girl knows how to lie. Look at her. She hated high school and kicked me back because I couldn't hide my laughter.

This dinner is a mess. What does Ummi see in this man? Money? He looked like he had none. Looks? He wasn't Denzel. Personality? Hmm. I'll pass. All I know was that he was trying way too hard to impress. Khadi is falling for it, but not me.

When dinner came, I finished quickly and went back to liking my friends' pictures on Instagram. I counted the minutes, but Ummi wasn't anywhere near from getting up.

"So, are we finished here?" I stood up, and it caught everyone off-guard.

"I'm done, are you, honey?" Maleek asked Ummi. I didn't look at her as my stare went straight to Khadi.

"You're finish, right?" I grabbed her hand. She nodded but didn't I remember why I was there. "I think it's time for us to talk, Maleek." I said grabbing my handbag.

"I agree, you ladies, please meet me at the car." He left a fifty-dollar bill on the table and ushered me to go in front of him. We went out a side exit of the restaurant about thirty meters from the car.

"To the point, what do you want with my mother?"

Maleek appeared shocked for my bluntness, but I didn't care.

"Our plans, you mean? We're getting married soon."

Just like that it felt like twenty daggers stabbed me in the heart, all at once. *"What in the world?"*

"Getting married? She said nothing about a marriage. Maybe she was talking about someone else." I laughed, not believing a word.

"We love each other, isn't that enough of a reason?" Maleek tried pleading with me. I couldn't go for his game. Not today.

"How can someone fall in love with somebody in two months? I'm not stupid. Before I left for work in Boston, my mom was in love with my father. Now, you just pop up."

"I did, Gabrielle. As much as it hurts you, I love your mother and I'm not afraid to admit it." He lowered his head, and I didn't know what to say. *Couldn't tell if he was telling the truth or straight up lying. Even if he was really in love with Ummi, wasn't rushing to get married over the top? Sheesh, it's only been two months.*

I looked at his body language before I replied. He

seems genuine. "Don't think you can ever take the place of my father."

"I could never. I just want to make your Ummi happy only by the Grace of Allah."

"Wow! What did she say to him?" I never heard such words. Not even from the boys who liked me. How is this coming from another man besides my father?

"Was she sad when she left my father?" I asked not knowing why I did. Ummi was good at hiding her pain.

"She was, and I was there at the right time to console her. We met in the office one day and since, we've been good friends."

I understood now. He wants to be the one who rescues her. Does Ummi think she owe this guy something? I guess she must make her own bed.

"Maleek, my father was a great man. I'm still pissed at the fact they got divorced, but Ummi deserves to be happy. I can't stand in her way. If you make her happy, I'm for it." My face was serious. I would see with time how he treats her, but for now, I'll give him a pass.

"*Billahi*, I promise Gabrielle, I'll take care of your mother regarding your father's honor."

I appreciated his words as much as I hate to admit it.

We walked back to the car and Maleek took us home. Once we got in, Khadi had some catching up to do on her homework, I went up to my room just and as I undressed, a text came on my phone stating: *We know you're here.*

GETTIN' WITH MY GIRLS

"Mom, I already told you, I will be out for a little while. I know it's Khadi's birthday." I explained, storming out of the house as she yelled on deaf ears. We were on better terms since the dinner two days ago. Maleek hasn't come around since, so I guess he was busy. I didn't mind him coming over, but not every day. As long as Ummi's happy, I am.

I took Ummi's car to Aisha's house who lived twenty minutes away. There were three cars parked in the driveway, so the rest of the girls were inside. There's a space across the street. *I got this.*

Khadi's birthday party is in exactly three hours. I got to be quick. The girls would be mad, but Ummi telling I'd be there was enough.

I stepped on Aisha's porch and rang the doorbell.

Her mother must have changed the facade, and it looked good. The brown color added a needed sign of life. The house went from looking like the oldest one on the block to the best.

Just when I was about to ring again, Aisha opened the door. "*Salam alaikum.* Oh my God, I missed you!" She embraced me tightly, barely leaving me to breathe. I laughed hugging her back, not sure what to say. We had beef before I left for Boston, but the girls apologized and now we were good.

"I missed you too," I mumbled, still in her embrace.

"Come on, let's go inside the girls are upstairs." I was having a panic attack walking upstairs, not knowing what to expect.

On the second floor, I saw my girls, laying on Aisha's bed, gossiping and laughing. "Gals, Gabbie's here!" All of them darted towards me, screaming. I put my hands over my ears. *There won't be much oxygen left.* I smiled, hugging them.

"We missed you so much, how you've been?" asked Aliyah sitting back down on the bed.

"Boston was something else. Those white people had it out for me the moment I arrived."

"What happened to the black girl magic, honey, did you have it?" Aliyah laughed so hard that she had tears. I shrugged and so were the others. *She's got the corniest of jokes.*

"Hmm, ok." I was puzzled.

Layla changed the subject. "You know that cute boy Khalil got one of us." She seemed jealous, judging from her posture. Layla was getting married after I left. Not sure what happened. She was so infatuated with that boy, you couldn't tell her nothing.

"Who's Khalil again?" I asked, as if I didn't know already.

"That boy, Layla wants to marry. She's gushing over him." Aliyah butted in, kicking Layla with her foot. Layla was quick to return the hit with a pillow. We laughed, and she continued. "I thought the curly head negro loved me you know. I didn't expect things to turn out this way. They were the best four months of my life."

She's exaggerating too much now. The girl always had brothers sweating her, talking about "Sis, who's your wakeel and etc.?" Don't know why she's hung up on him. I guess I'll never get it.

"He wasn't the one for you, girl. There are plenty of brothers in Pakistan for you," joked Aisha. Everyone laughed and Layla didn't enjoy being the butt of them.

"Negative and next," she replied.

———

When we were in high school, we always had chats about these guys and their petty games. Usually after school, we'd drive around in Aisha's car through New York for hours, venting about how this brother and that one tried to get in our panties. I miss those conversations. Too bad, those days were long gone, but at least we still have the memories.

"So, is someone else cuffed in here?" I asked, playfully. Aliyah and Layla looked at Aisha.

"Aisha? The most reserved one in the house got who?"

"I just wanted to do my thing, you know. It's not all that deep. I don't even think we are made for each other. It's been eight weeks and we still don't know each other's phone number."

"Who's bae?"

Aisha looked at me, scared to answer. "Someone from my job, y'all don't know him."

Aliyah and Layla avoided looking at me as Aisha spoke.

"Well, we'll find out soon. Ain't we?" I pressed further. There's something up they aren't telling me.

"Yeah, sure."

"There will be a party at his place on Thursday.

We will be turning it up, there!" said Layla excited. I hoped they would and not me. I wasn't trying to get caught up in their foolishness. They looked at me as if I was supposed to say something.

"I'm not saying anything."

"Gabbie!" I tried ignoring Aisha, but the girls were expecting me to say something.

"I'm not going. I got a lot of catching up to do."

The girls' faces turned from bright to midnight.

"Why not?" said Aliyah.

"I'm too old for these parties. Ain't y'all tired of the same ole men there?"

They groaned.

"You're coming. I don't care. Even I have to hire you a man," said Layla acting like she was the boss. I shook my head in disbelief.

"I've decided a long time ago not to get mixed up with young boys. They ain't got nothing for me." I said, crossing my arms.

"Oh, come on, Stop acting like an old woman. You're only 22." pleaded Aisha taking my hand.

"You always say that, and then I end up playing y'all games and some fuck boy be trying to get in my panties. If it's meant to be with someone, they'll come along, I'm done with these girly men."

"Oh, no she didn't," said Layla.

"Just leave her. Gabbie'll be whining at thirty when she's home with fifteen cats," said Aliya sarcastically.

I couldn't believe this chick. "*And you'll be stuck married with five kids," I thought.*

"Well, think about it at least, Gabbie. It'll be a fun. Plus, you know we can't go without you."

I looked at my watch. "Oh shoot, I need to go." I had forty minutes till Khadi's birthday party.

"It's Khadi's birthday. I'd invite you, but Ummi said it's for her closest friends at school." I was surprised Ummi let Khadi have a party. She never let us do anything like this ever. When Dad was around, he wasn't having it. Now, Ummi's feeling herself with this Maleek thing. I cringed at the thought of the word 'party' as I left out of Aisha's home. "Salam alaikum, girls."

11

KHADI'S BIRTHDAY (SMH)

It took me twenty-five minutes to get from Brooklyn Heights back to our home. There were already cars piled up in our driveway. *How big was this damn party going to be again?* Khadi tried her best to fit in and sometimes did too much. Perhaps, Ummi thought this was a good idea for her to make new friends. Ummi, I guess cared about those friendships considering she was popular in high school. She didn't want us to be friendless. The negative was she was called in to work at the last minute, meaning I would be stuck babysitting the trapsters.

When I walked through the front door, there a few teenagers seated in the living room while others were chatting in the kitchen. The DJ was setting up his equipment and waved when he saw me. *Why are these youngsters here so early?* I looked around trying to spot Khadi, but she was nowhere in sight. *Where is she?*

I tapped the back of a girl sitting on the couch that went to Khadi's school. "Have you seen my sister? You know the birthday girl?" She shook her head, "No" and went back to talking with her friend. I went upstairs to find her and did so, in my bedroom.

"What are you doing in here?" *This girl is putting on my makeup.*

"You scared me, geez. Getting ready." She smiled, checking herself out in the mirror. "So, Ummi left you on watch, right?"

This girl thinks she is grown. "Khadi, you're turning seventeen not twenty-one, chill out." I plopped on the bed. "No drugs, weed, opioids or whatever else y'all youngsters do these days. I'm not ya'll babysitter."

"Ok."

"Don't just say okay. Remember, if anyone breaks something, this party is over." I snapped my fingers.

"Gosh! I know Gabbie. Ummi said the same thing, but I can't be in charge and have fun at the same time."

I understood her clearly, but Khadi must make sure nothing goes wrong. I won't be taking a trip to IKEA for new furniture tomorrow. It's just not happening.

"I'm glad you do." I glanced at my phone and opened Facebook. *Oh my God! Yunus, Aisha's boyfriend sent me a friend request. Interesting? How did he know who I am?* I didn't click accept right away and checked out his profile. This boy is a straight player.

All his photos just showed him hanging out with different ladies and friends. He was a show-off, flexing his muscles in front of luxury cars. I could puke. *Let's chill on this Facebook thing for a bit.* I ignored the request and saw Khadi had left out the room.

I groaned as I knew would be hard controlling these teens tonight. Some would drink off the pain. Not me. I'm Muslim. Downstairs, the party was already becoming packed. Khadi didn't know half of these teenagers. It's her party and choice as long as they don't mess up things. I worked my way between the teens and headed towards the kitchen where some were rolling up blunts in the corner.

"What y'all doing? Not in here. Take that somewhere else," I yelled.

"Ok." they yelled walking away.

There were empty beer cans on the kitchen table. *Oh my God! Ummi found out, she would lose her mind.* I cleared it off and headed to the DJ, telling him to stop the music. "Give me the mic." "Hey, y'all. Take y'all drinks, pills and smoking somewhere far away from this house or party is over." Many laughed, but when I changed my facial expression, they said

"Okay". Even some yelled, "Ok, Mom Dukes." *These kids gonna make me hurt them.*

The music resumed, making my ears deaf. More teens were coming through the door, and it didn't look like there was any more space. I could barely breathe. The least I wanted right now was one of these young boys trying to grind on my booty. One came up looking like he wanted some. I put my hand up and walked away.

I keep moving through the crowd, but the large amount of sweaty bodies kept pushing and pushing me backwards. My top priority was keeping Khadi safe. *Hold up—wait a minute!*

She's over there dancing with a guy holding a red cup. I snapped two pictures of her grinding on the guy like a hooker. *What a mess!* Once Ummi sees this, she'll be grounded for a year. The wonderful thought of blackmailing Khadi delighted me.

Was I evil? Maybe, but I'm just helping her in life by teaching her a lesson or two. "Khadi sweetheart, I think that's enough." I yanked her, leaving the thirsty boy dancing alone. "What the hell?" he protested trying to grab hold of my sister.

"Back off or else you can leave!"

He mumbled something and left.

"These kids got me in my bag tonight."

Khadi pulled away from me and went on dancing with a group of girls. I sighed crossing my arms, watching her closely.

When I left to the living room, there were teens dancing on the coffee table. I snapped out. "Get the hell down now!" I yelled, and they seemed terrified. *Making a scene, I didn't really care. This babysitter thing is irking the hell out of me.*

I sat in a space on the couch and peeped over across the room, seeing two kids making out. "What the hell y'all doin' over there? Go to y'all homes with that." They got up and sighed. Let's open Facebook and see what's up with Aisha and Yunus. I ignored the teens for a few minutes and read through their posts.

"Two *months together happy anniversary!*" posted Aisha.

I laughed while seeing Yunus' friend request still pending. I accepted, so I could see more posts on him. He had cute pictures of him and Aisha together on Facebook which was the total opposite of his Instagram account.

Aisha looked happy. They were smiling in almost every picture I scrolled down. All his posts was only with her on his feed which was weird. Maybe he got a burner account. *It's not of my business.*

I kept searching downwards, but then a distant crash snapped me out of my thoughts. Everybody was cheering, and I got up to see what was going on. Someone broke our back window in the kitchen.

Boiling in anger, it didn't take much until I lost it. "Everybody out—now!" I yelled, pushing kids towards the exit. People booed and kept booing, but I kept on exploding.

"Can't you people hear me!? Get out of my house!" I yelled on the mic when the DJ turned off the music. The crowd let themselves out while I walked towards the window to inspect it. Ummi will be pissed. I need to get this fixed before she comes home later. Khadi wanted to have this party, but she was doing her own thing. Matter of fact where is she anyway?

"Khadi," I yelled. The crowd was clearing out, and I ran upstairs to see if she was there. I opened my bedroom, no one. Then, I went to Ummi's room and saw a couple on the bed, making out, half-naked.

"Didn't you hear me from downstairs? Everybody out!"

The girl and boy quickly put on their clothes. I groaned and went to Khadi's bedroom. *Oh, my God!*

She was laying there with an older boy, on top of her about to have sex.

I pushed him off her and slapping him. My hand was in pain, as a result.

"What the fuck?" He yelled, holding his cheek.

"Out of my house, you damn dog. Don't you know I can call the cops? She's underage."

He apologized and left grabbing his clothes. Khadi was embarrassed and shaking.

"Why this, sister?" I was disappointed.

"I wanted to try it. My friends talk about sex all the time."

"Are you stupid or what? You have your whole life ahead of you and you want to waste it on this lame ass duck. We're Muslims. We save ourselves for our husbands. Ummi and Abee didn't raise us this way."

"Sorry, sister. It will never happen again. Please don't tell Abee and Ummi. They will kill me."

"I'll think about. I got pictures of you and that guy holding the red cup. If you do it again, I'll show them to Ummi. Now, you must help me clean up the house. Your friends tore it up."

"Ok, I promise."

The house smelled like weed and alcohol. I opened the windows, and Khadi picked up the trash everywhere. I went back downstairs, sighing that all of this was on my shoulders. Ummi texted me saying that her and Maleek were at his mother's house in Rochester. She'll be gone for tonight. When she comes home tomorrow and see that window, Khadi and I will be in big trouble. I picked up the broken glass in the kitchen and almost cut myself. The only I could do about the window until the morning was take a piece of cardboard from the shed and cover it up.

12

BIG TROUBLE

"I knew I couldn't trust you to be in charge. Look at this mess!" Ummi was yelling at me and Khadi as she surveyed the broken window. It was a scary thing when she got mad; I got goosebumps whenever she did.

I told her there were too many freaking kids. Khadi couldn't believe I didn't solely take the blame. *I should rat on her.*

"Umm, I didn't see who did it. What can I do to make it right?" Khadi whined, frowning.

"You wanna make it right, huh? Maybe grounding you for the month. I think that is appropriate."

I tried my best not to laugh. Khadi's facial expression was too priceless not to.

"Stop laughing at me." I raised my eyebrows, challenging her to dare speak. What's she going to say? I had all the evidence I need against her, anyway.

"Oh, by the way, Gabrielle. I ran into Aliyah on my way here. She said she would call you to go out or something," said Ummi passing by. *If it was about that damn party, I wasn't interested.*

Aliyah had no plans for her future. She only cared about partying and being seen. Definitely wasn't where I was. But who am I to judge?

"Let me call the window people to get this fixed before the thieves come. To your room, Khadi."

"Mom!"

"Ok, Ummi." I said snickering under my breath.

"And make sure you call Aliyah. Don't just stay at home, Gabbie. Go have fun for once. You need a break."

"Ok."

Khadi stomped upstairs to her room while Ummi came back with the Yellow Pages. She made coffee while looking for a window store.

"So, how's Maleek?"

Ummi cleared her throat and got up to get coffee.

"He's all right. His mother is having a lot of

medical problems these days along with some other drama."

"What drama?"

"She doesn't like our relationship because I have children. I guess I'm not good enough for him in her eyes."

"What kind of mother would even say that? You don't need her approval for happiness. Do what makes you happy."

Ummi turned, smiling. I smiled back giving her a quick wink. "Everything will be fine, Ma. I think he loves you." I grabbed a mug and poured a little coffee for myself. As I was doing so, I thought about Abee. I didn't want to ask her why they separated and spoil this moment.

"I knew it would be hard for you to accept," said Ummi.

I didn't know what to say, but I just couldn't get over the pain of my parents being divorced. Maleek knew he would never replace my Abee, but if he works hard enough, he'd be a good second one. Perhaps I'll be long gone working in another state by then.

"Okay, enough I might cry. Did you get text Aliyah yet?" Ummi got up to wash dishes.

"Nope, the girls are going to a party Wednesday night. Not sure if I'm gonna go."

"You should. You need to go out. These years while you are single are so precious. You'll never have them again."

Maybe, she was right. I had the stay-home bug almost always.

"All right, you got me. I will call Aliyah and see what's going on." I felt bad and went upstairs to my room. "Just lay down and relax," my mind kept telling me.

What would I miss if I stayed home? I checked my text messages, nothing, as usual. I didn't text Aliyah back, but as soon as I opened Snapchat, my phone rang. It was Aisha.

I sat up. "Hey. *Salam alaikum*, Sis."

"*Wa alaikum As-Salam*. Get ready, we're going to the mall in an hour!" She sounded excited.

"The mall? For what?" I said annoyingly.

"Layla and Aliyah just wanna hang out. Come on, I heard that you needed some new clothes." *I opened my mouth in shock, my clothes? Who? Probably one of those teenagers from the party. She's talking real fly. The girl's clothes needed to be thrown out and set on fire, not mine.*

"Fine, come pick me up in an hour?"

"Ok, I'm already ready. Just waiting on Aliyah and

Layla. You know how they are. I'll probably be there in two."

"Okay then, I'll be ready."

"Ok. *Masalama*." Aisha hung up. I took out one of my best outfits from the closet, pondering on what did I just get myself into.

After a long shower and blow drying my hair to make the curls pop, Khadi came in, grinning. "I see you're going out?"

"Yeah, to the mall."

"Wow, about damn time. I will write this down in my journal."

I grabbed my brush, ready to throw it at her. She ran out of my room yelling "Ummi." *What a rascal.* Ummi spoiled that brat while my dad didn't. But as Khadi got older, she got big-headed.

I did a little makeup, for the first time in a while and it brought out my tannish skin. *Damn, I'm looking good.*

An hour passed since Aisha called, and I was bored, so I went into Khadi's room to see what she was up to and as usual, the girl was taking selfies, laying on her bed.

"Aren't you tired of that? Damn, you be updating your profile picture every day?"

She was trying so hard to be liked. It was hilarious.

"Oh my God! What are you wearing? And from what thrift store did you get it from?"

I hit her with one of her pillows. "H&M, thank you very much and for your information it's looks good."

"Yeah, if you're a sixty with no man." I rolled my eyes. Why did I even bother coming in on her? Khadi was having fun at my expense. I was about to say something but before I could, my phone rang. It's Aisha, again.

"Salam alaikum," I said, shushing my sister who was mumbling something.

"Come downstairs. We're in front." Aisha was laughing at something that Aliyah and Layla said.

"Ok."

THE MALL EPISODE

Aisha was driving her dad's car. "Why is she waving at me like that?" *We saw each other a few days ago. Anyway.* Aliyah and Layla were chatting and ignored me until I got inside the car.

"Your outfit is cute," said Aliyah sucking on a lollipop.

"*Shukran, Sis.*"

Layla was in the back, on the phone with somebody. She didn't even bother to give me the salaams.

As Aisha pulled off, I knew from that moment I wouldn't have a good time.

"So, what are you planning on getting at the mall?" I asked Aisha.

"I need something new for the party on Wednesday."

"My feet hurt from my shoes. I think I'm outgrowing them. We need to stop at the DKNY store, too," added Aliyah.

I sighed. *Damn! We might be at the mall all day.*

"Great, I need more makeup. Seriously. My collection is going dry because I don't have the proper concealer," said Layla pissed about something.

"Ya Allah, I can't believe this. This girl was supposed to do my hair Wednesday morning and now she can't." Layla threw her phone in her bag, leaning against the window. *This girl is so dramatic.*

"There are hundreds of hairstylists in New York. You'll live," said Aisha taking the words right out of my mouth.

"This girl does my hair the best. If I go to someone else, they'll messed it up."

This conversation made me think about what happened last year when we got into so many fights. These three ended up ignoring me and bad-mouthing me to others. I'm over it, since they apologized. It saddened me they were backbiting me to some sisters, but I had to let it go and put my trust in Allah.

———

Aisha pulled up to the mall's parking lot. Everyone

said that they were thirsty. "Just get out of my car. We're going to Starbucks," said Aisha.

"I hope they're not still profiling people. Hey, I might have to use the restroom before I buy something," said Layla. We laughed so hard that people passing by us thought we were crazy. The sun was out shining, unlike what I saw while I was in Boston.

The mall was packed. While waiting on our drinks, Layla and Aliyah were checking out some boys coming inside. "I wonder if they Muslim."

"Those beards. Damn' they look sexy," blurted Aisha though she's engaged to Yunus or supposed to be, anyway.

"Finally," gasped Layla when they called our names for our drinks. Starbucks was packed, so Layla suggested we headed over to Forever 21.

I walked beside Aisha while Aliyah walked with Layla. The clothes we tried on were too small or too tight. There were a few pieces I liked, but as usual I was being me. *Ummi told me to have a good time, remember?*

"Do you like this?" Aisha pointed at a flower-printed blouse, perfect for the summer vibe of this year.

"It's cute. Try it on?"

"I—"

"Go ahead, girl." She took it off the rack and went to the changing room. While she was trying on the outfit, I walked up to Layla and Aliyah, to see what they were up to.

They were talking about something but soon as they saw me; they stopped and changed the subject. *Why did I even come along? They keep doing this nonsense.*

"What were you guys talking about?" They thought I wouldn't ask.

"O-oh just this top," said Aliyah. "I should try it on."

I could read right through them. "Yeah, it's pretty, go try it on."

The top Layla was holding was ugly as hell. They looked at each other as Layla went to the fitting room. A few seconds later, Aisha came out, wearing the flowery blouse.

"How do I look?" she said, smiling.

"You go, girl. Oh, my God! You should get it." I'm being honest. Aliyah gave the thumbs up.

"I guess I'll get it!" Aisha was happy. While she went to change, I looked around the store at some blouses. I wanted to get something, just for the heck.

After I circled the blouse section a few times and

noticed Aisha heading towards the checkout counter. Layla and Aliyah weren't with her.

Aisha paid and then walked towards me with the most priceless smile ever. Once she saw I wasn't with Layla and Aliyah, her smile faded. "Where are they?"

"I didn't see where they went."

"We should call them."

She pulled out her phone first, worried. "Where y'all at?" She asked, looking in the exit's direction.

"Okay, I see you never mind."

"Why did you leave?" I asked acting concerned.

"One of Layla's friends called. It was too much noise inside," explained Aliyah.

"Oh, was it someone we know?" asked Aisha.

"No, my manager from work. I'm doing a double this Friday," complained Layla and from the look on her face, I think I believe her.

Layla and Aliyah had a way of twisting their words. At some point, it becomes a little over the top. "Anyway, let's go to another store, I'm sure you can find something there, Gabbie." Aisha grabbed my hand and led me out. There was a store with a banner hanging that read, *New in Town - Debbie's.* Everything looked expensive inside but there were markups posted every-where on the front window.

"Let's see what Debbie's has. Maybe you can find some shoes, Aliyah" said Aisha. Aliyah was gushing about the sales on shoes they displayed as we came inside.

"This store looks out of place, don't you think?" I told Aisha, who was too busy looking at everything. She motioned for me to hush. *What's her deal?*

She came beside me. "There are rumors about the owners of this store being part of the Italian mafia. I'm not sure if it's true. Don't miss out on these deals from Italy!" Aisha chuckled as she went through the store.

"Come here, Gabbie. Look at this."

"I don't like that one."

"How about this one?" Aisha took a top off the racks, which looked like an audition outfit for a sex worker.

"Aisha, I'd never wear this." I took a hold of the blouse and put it back.

"Oh, come on. You need to live your best life, girl for just a moment." She grinned handing me the top and pointing at the fitting rooms.

"Are you crazy? I'm not trying this on. My mother would kill me if I wore something like this." I said handing it back to her.

While Aisha and I were arguing about the shirt, an old woman behind her was saying something. "What are you doing—?" she said.

"What did you say?" I asked coming closer.

"I said what are you doing with that blouse?"

"Nothing, I'm trying to get my friend to try it on." Aisha explained joining me. Layla and Aliyah then appeared, listening in. I peeked to look behind her and saw two men coming out of a room, watching us. They didn't look like security.

"I don't think so. Just trying on clothes and not buying. You ladies have something else in mind?" said the woman with her arms crossed while the men looked on.

"Excuse me, what do you mean?" *Was she accusing us of stealing? These people were in the back the whole time watching us like criminals. It was nonsense she's implying we were trying to steal a ten-dollar top.*

"I saw one of you put something in your bag. The censors will go off the second you step out." She signaled to the men to come. *I couldn't believe it. Seriously?*

"Are you serious? We didn't take anything. We were just browsing like the rest of the people in the mall." Aisha returned the top in its rack, trying to erase any misunderstanding.

"Is there a problem here, ladies?" A security guard came up after walking with the two men watching us.

"This lady right here just accused us of shoplifting because we are black. I think she's a racist," said Aisha.

"How dare you? I work here, sweetheart and I'm not a racist. I also know that my eyes don't deceive me."

"Listen Ma'am, I don't know what your problem is, but it's not us. We ain't do nothing," said Aliyah.

"Girls, you need to open your bags," demanded the security guard.

"I don't see a reason why I should open anything. You've got to be crazy. This lady is profiling us because we are Black and Muslim and so you are too!" There were a few whites in the store, looking at us as if we were criminals.

Then, the guard had the audacity to grab mine. I yanked it back and when I did so; he reached for his gun. "Oh, so now you're gonna shoot me? Is that what's this is all about?" I yelled, not caring.

I caught everyone's attention, and now a small group of shoppers gathered in front of the store to see what was going on.

"You need to calm down, Miss. I'm only doing my job," said the security guard.

"I'm sure, murder is not part of your job description. Is it?"

Aisha nudged me to shut up and stepped in front of me. This girl thinks she will protect me, but I knew I how to hold my own. *Don't come this way with the BS.*

"It's just a misunderstanding here." Aisha grabbed my bag with full force and gave it to the security guard.

"Aisha!"

"Are you trying to get yourself killed?"

I shook my head, looking. The guard went to the counter and opened the bag, rummaging through it.

"Shut up and stay silent." Aisha turned around and gave them a fake smile.

The guard then looked at us before turning around and giving a nod to the men standing beside the woman.

"Oh my God! No, you didn't" said Aliyah.

"I didn't take nothing."

"Shit! Why didn't you give him the bag when he first asked then?" remarked Layla, pissed.

"It's mine. What am I supposed to do?"

As we were arguing, two men came up to us, and one spoke in a very strong accent. "Ladies, I think you need to come with us and give us your cellphones." The black suits they were wearing made them look intimidating, but their facial expressions signaled otherwise.

"We did nothing wrong. There's no reason for us to

come with you, you damn creeps. And you're not getting my phone!" I said.

"This isn't a question. Our boss here saw you taking a shirt." A different man ignored my protests, and it was obvious the other one beside him agreed. *Something was going on and it wasn't because of us. This cheap ass clothing shop is up to something.*

"She can't see. Look at her bifocals. Does she even know who you are? It's clear she's singling us out," screamed Aliyah, who was probably the most nervous amongst us.

"You aren't in no position to make such claims, now follow us and give us your fucking phones, NOW! or we will have problems here," yelled a fat man in a black tight suit.

We complied taking our phones out of our bags. Then, one man grabbed Layla, pulling her towards the back room. Right before we could say yell, some others came and pushed us back there too.

The woman who accused us went back to counter, saying to the customers, "Sorry for the trouble. We've caught shoplifters. The store will close because of this unfortunate event."

———

As they seated us in a strange room, I started mentally making comparisons of what it resembled; a gas chamber, maybe a prison cell, hmm.., a torture chamber, etc. The gates of the store could be heard closing, and the lights from outside the door appear to dim. They told us to wait. Layla and Aliyah turned; their redbone faces were red.

"This is all your fault, you should've tried on the top," said Aliyah pouting. I didn't know which I could despise most, her voice or her words?

"Ya Allah" and then I answered, "This isn't because of me. They had their eyes on us the first minute we walked inside."

"Right, spare me the BS. I shopped here before with no problems." Aliyah rolled her eye, tapping her foot nervous as hell.

"Maybe if you would apologize, Gabbie. We'll feel better." Layla popped her head behind Aliyah's, looking at me, poking out her lips.

"Look, I have no reason to apologize. I didn't take anything."

Aisha quickly interrupted our airing-out session. "Everyone shut up." Her eyes were on another room to the right. We saw the foot shadows and a lot of talking in foreign accents.

We'll never make it home. We're going to get whacked in this fake ass department store.

"Aliyah, what do you know about this store?" I asked.

"Not much, there were rumors from some of my friends, the guy who owns it is some mafia boss."

"Why would a mafia boss own a cheap-ass store like this?" said Aisha, believing every word that came out of Aliyah's mouth.

"Freakin' geniuses. Why not? It's the perfect place to hide your dirt," I said.

Aisha looked scared as ever believing everything. "Yo! Look, there's a red exit light over there. Maybe it will lead us outside where we can run for our lives?"

"Let's see," said Layla. As we walked towards it, the door where we were standing opened. An Italian man was holding a big gun dressed in a black suit, looked at us, not saying anything. Next to him, was a woman wearing a white hat with brunette hair holding the same gun. "This must be his mistress," I thought. The man reminded me of someone in Goodfellas.

"I guess you're our special guests or special victims this afternoon," he said smiling while Layla was the only idiot, popping bubble gum, smiling back. The girl looked like she wanted to flirt with him.

"Don't do this now," I thought. *We're in deep shit*

and this girl is acting dumb as hell. Sheesh, I hope Ummi doesn't find us in New York Harbor. The worst-case scenarios ran through my head, but escaping didn't appear to be an option.

"Look sir, we didn't take anything. That lady accused us of taking that cheap shirt. I doubt if she can see anything," said Aisha which shocked us. The girl never stands up for anything. Meanwhile, the Italian man and woman weren't impressed.

"Take them to my office. I have a few questions," the man ordered. Without hesitation, the men in black suits pushed us forward.

"Get your slimy hands off of me. I know Karate," I yelled pulling away.

———

The Italian man's office was more arranged than where they were holding us. The guards pushed us down on a leather sofa which appeared to cost thousands of dollars. Aisha began talking first, and I couldn't even look the man and woman in the eyes.

"Sir, I'm sure we can clear up this misunderstanding." Then, she was interrupted. "I don't appreciate you girls coming inside my store and stealing my property." His hands and gun were in full view as he sat his desk and a woman was standing above him. *I guess he was expecting us to admit our guilt.*

"We weren't stealing anything. We were just shopping. Look at the cameras. That lady was targeting us from the minute we came inside." I spoke up. Again, he cut me off. "That lady is my mother, and I'm sure I'd trust her more than you ever."

His mother? Sheesh, we're now in deep shit. If he was such a powerful man why would his mother be working at this store? Anyway, I'll reserve my thoughts for another time.

After a few moments of silence, the woman, who we thought was simply an employee, entered the room.

"I suggest you check the security cameras, sir. Obviously, your mother's mistaken. I know my friends," said Aisha. That was the most courageous thing I ever heard from her.

"I'm confused. How is this store making money, anyway? Sales signs all over the place and nobody's buying," added Aliyah.

The man loaded his gun, and his mother and the other lady looked furious. *Oh, shit! My janaza is all I thought of. Homegirl ain't gonna make it, and neither will my girls.*

"It's not every day, we get a group of lovely ladies like yourselves visiting us and having an interest in buying clothes." His words made sure we knew he was the boss, and he wasn't talking about the department store. "You seem to know a lot about my operation, young lady?"

"No, no, sir. Just the gossip."

"You're right, Ricardo, honey. This is not a store where our customers come to play around. It's for business only," said the woman standing above him in a deep Italian accent.

"We want no trouble, sir. We apologize if we did something wrong. Please, our parents are waiting for us to come home," pleaded Layla sounding desperate. As she got up, but one guard walked to her side, with his hand on his gun.

"If you don't sit your ass down girl," whispered Aisha. "Are you saying we are thieves, sir? Not all Black people are doing badly."

"If you're at the point where you want to steal a ten-dollar shirt, then yes. Maybe you on Opioids, weed, or any drug. Who's knows? Why should I give a fuck? I have a business to run and you have cost me time in losing money this afternoon." His facial expression turned serious but his mother was grinning. *What a strange sight!*

"In all honesty, my girl would never wear that top you have in your hands. It looks like something that

Hillary Clinton would wear. My girl ain't about looking like a politician," said Aliyah. *It's true, but why is she dissing me?*

Somehow, that made everyone in the room laugh. "Goody two shoes, never expected to see someone like that at my store." The man said reclining in his chair.

"By the way, are you hiring? I don't have a job at the moment," Layla said playing with her khimar. *This girl's gonna make me slap the black off her. They could kill us right now.*

"We are not at the moment. We have all the help we need," said the woman standing behind the man said.

"The help?" The man laughed so hard that his mother told him to cut it out.

"Ok, all jokes aside. My friend's telling the truth. Gabrielle's one of the most honest people I've ever known. If she wanted to steal something, it would be from Victoria's Secret to be honest with you."

How could Layla deliver a low blow like that? She must think this is fun and games. Our lives are at stake and my fashion choices ain't that bad.

"Well, it looks like maybe you are telling the truth. Our cameras haven't caught you." The man said after looking at his phone. "Are you sure you are friends?"

"Al hamdulilah," sighed Aisha.

Layla laughed, nodding. "Gabbie's the ugly duckling in our friend club. We can't even find her a mate."

Everyone in the room laughed including his mother. I was pissed and couldn't believe Layla was roasting me. *Just keep your composure, girl. You got this.* Aisha patted me on the back. "Everything will be okay." I looked back with a slight grin.

"So, let's just call this a misunderstanding." He grabbed the gun off the table and put it back in his desk. "You're free to go, ladies. Think before going around. Not all places are meant to be playgrounds." The man got up from his chair and exited the room with his mother and the other woman.

"Ok, sir," said Aisha.

"Hey, Joey! Give the ladies 25% off of future purchases. Will ya?"

"Yes, sir." The fat guard handed us some vouchers and showed us to the exit.

We were left in a trance about what just happened. Never did I think I'd experience something crazier than Boston.

We left the store arguing about how I felt offended by Layla and Aliyah's jokes. They said they had to do it.

"Those Italians like Black people's jokes, my dad

always told me. I'm sorry, Sis, but I had to or they would have killed us."

"No problem."

We kept looking back to see if anyone was following us as we were quickly exiting to the parking lot. In our minds, were memories of how the mobsters used to whack their targets in the most unusual of spots. When we left, the mall appeared to be nearing closing time.

14

IT'S ALL GOOD

I checked myself in the front mirror. This was as good as it could get. I sighed, taking Ummi's car keys and fixing my hair. It's been exactly five days since our ordeal and the girls and I tried to forget about it. I couldn't tell Ummi or she'd have a heart attack.

It's Wednesday, and I'm going to Aisha's house to her party. Yes, I got myself to go. I gave salaams to Maleek and Ummi and was on my out the door. There wasn't much traffic, and I got to Aisha's in about fifteen minutes.

There's hardly anyone outside. I must be one of the first to show up. The front door was open and there were several boys with Ma sitting on the couch, looking at TV. The DJ was setting up the equipment and a few of Aisha's cousins were decorating the house.

"Have y'all seen Aisha?"

"She's upstairs getting ready," Ma said after exchanging salaams with me. I didn't recognize the boys there but there was a cute one amongst them. *Maybe Aisha has more friends than all of us.*

Aisha was in front of the mirror, getting ready. "Hey girl. *Salam alaikum.*" She hugged me. "*Wa alaikum as Salam.* I'm glad you came here first. This party's gonna be lit!"

"I thought I was running late. God! My mind's still on the Italians. I don't want Joey and the crew to come whack us, you know?"

"It's all over, girl. Just chill out," laughed Aisha, as she was doing her hair.

"Who are those boys downstairs with your mom?"

"Oh, they're Yunus' buddies. They're good."

I looked around her room, like I haven't seen the place a hundred times before.

"So, where's Yunus, then?" I joked.

"He'll come by later after work. Dude's working a lot these days trying to save money for our marriage."

Yeah, right," I thought.

As Aisha finished up, I looked at my phone and didn't realize Aisha was standing in front of me, holding a bag.

What's this, "Aisha? It's not my birthday." I looked puzzled by its shape.

"Just open it, Gabbie." It was the same top we got accused of stealing.

"Oh my God! You aren't serious? I know you didn't steal it, did you? You trying to get us killed."

"No, silly. I bought it with the voucher when I went back to the mall yesterday."

Honestly, I hated it but and hated every memory associated with it.

"Wear it and take that old one off you're wearing."

"It's cute. I'm not wearing that. Who knows if they will show up to the party?"

"Come on, now. I got the receipt. What you're wearing is cute for my grandma. Go on and change."

I stuck out my tongue as I walked to the bathroom. Aisha was nice enough to buy me this, and the shirt wasn't so bad as I kept looking at it in the mirror. "Just for tonight, Gabbie, you're gonna be all right," I said looking at my stomach. "I'm getting fat." The blouse didn't feel comfortable, but I couldn't lie I looked good in it.

"Are you done yet?" yelled Aisha, outside the bathroom door.

"Just a second!" I fixed my hair and evened out my concealer. Moments later, she saw me and gasped.

"What have you been hiding for all these years?" With her mouth open, Aisha walked towards me, checking me out.

"Oh stop it, I don't feel good. I'm getting fat."

"You look good, girl. You need to have a little confidence." It feels good to be complimented.

"Okay enough talking, everyone's downstairs waiting for us." Aisha pushed me ahead.

"Waiting for you, not me. These people don't even know me."

———

The party had started, and the music was lit. There were some local rappers who came through but only one of them had bars. It was more crowded than Khadi's party and Aisha greeted everyone. I stood by her side and was approached by many boys.

"Where you get that shirt from, girl?" One girl asked staring at me. "That shirt's dope. It brings out your whole figure."

"My friend got it for me from—I don't know exactly." *Damn shame, I can't even say where.*

Layla and Aliyah walked through the front door as if they were VIPs. *Drama queens as usual.* I stood by

Aisha's side watching them hugged everyone. Aisha and I went to the kitchen to get something to eat.

After their little intro, Aliyah and Layla walked in, gasping for air. "What did you do to our Gabrielle? That shirt is—" said Layla.

"Oh, my God! You stole it for real? Didn't you?" said Aliyah.

"No, dummy. Aisha bought it with the voucher. Y'all crazy!"

Aliyah swirled around me, complimenting every my figure. "Girl, got hips. Look at her."

"Gabs, honestly, you look amazing. I knew you'd pull off looking good in that shirt," said Layla.

"Thank you, Layla, you look good as always." *She looked different, which I liked. Her outfit wasn't anything over the top for the first time. Was she finally coming to her senses?*

The girls and I indulged in a genuine conversation, laughing together and for the first time in a while, it felt real.

"We need to go shopping again. Sheesh, it was so much fun!" said Aisha.

"Hell! No!" I blurted.

"Oh, shoot! Look! Here comes Yunus," said Aliyah.

"How's my future wife doing?" He wrapped his

arms around Aisha and kissed her cheek. He came in looking like he had drip; all fresh for this little party.

"I missed you."

"Hi Aliyah. Layla." He greeted them with the salaams and then stopped when he reached me. "I never seen you around before? Are you Gabrielle?"

"Yeah, I was up away at school and then I went up to Boston."

Yunus' eyebrows raised. "Hmm, I've heard a lot about you. It's nice to finally meet you." *His player mentality wouldn't fool me, but it was none of my business. I will say that Yunus was cute in person.*

"Thank you. The pleasure is mine."

―――――

The party went well and as soon as it was 2 AM; I was time for me to get up out. Without arguing for once, we had a good time, and the party was lit.

At home, Ummi and Khadi were asleep. I went to bed finally in peace.

The next morning, I was in the kitchen, making myself something to eat and Ummi laughed when she came inside.

"Good morning, salaam alaikum."

"Wa alaikum as salaam. What's so funny, Umm? You've been laughing since you saw me."

"You with that top on. I never thought I'd see you wear that in my lifetime."

"Oh, snap!" I looked down at my chest. "I must have forgotten to take it off when I came in."

"Maleek's coming over soon. We want to talk about you about something before I tell Khadi."

"I'll be here. It must be serious?"

"Not really, but I'll let you decide when he gets here." Ummi smiled. I think I know what was up and would support her, regardless.

Khadi came downstairs, almost ready to go to school, looking out of her mind.

"What's up with you and that top? You look like you about to work in Vegas."

"Just stop it, girl. It was a present from Aisha." I tried covering it up while Ummi was laughing.

"Right, right." Khadi giggled as she came closer. I was hiding my chest with an apron and was ready to hit her.

"Gabrielle, leave your sister alone and Khadi, make sure you have everything for school. I'll have breakfast for you in a few minutes."

"Ok, Ummi." She went to the living room to watch TV.

Ten minutes later, Maleek parked in front of the house and came inside.

"*Salam alaikum.* Hey, ladies!" He said with a huge smile.

"This guy thinks he's in. Don't he?" I thought.

He sat down next to my mother and hugged her. I did our best not to vomit, but I'd be lying if I said their little relationship wasn't cute.

"So, you need to tell us something?" My knees buckled, already expecting the news. Ummi looked at him and then at us.

"Well, Gabrielle. Your mother and I will be getting married this weekend." As those words left his mouth, Khadi came inside the kitchen and caught the conversation. She jumped up, pumping her fists while I couldn't hold back my tears for Ummi. What a joy!

"Congratulations, I know you'll make my mom happy, Maleek." I smiled and stood up to embrace him, finally. Ummi will be happily married and Khadi will finish out high school in a few months.

As for me, I'd try my hand at another job and try to stay out of trouble. Who knows if that's possible?

THERE AND NOW

VOLUME ONE

LIL E IN THE CRIB

CHAPTER ONE

I'm Lil E, the youngster who made it out of North Philly to tell this story you are now reading. 1975's summer heat was blazing. I was living with my mom and grandparents in a second-floor apartment on Tenth and Susquehanna Avenue and remember the fan that was blowing hot air through my grandma's bedroom window. Despite only being two years old, I have a few memories of that time period.

Pop-Pop (my grandfather) would hold me while Grandma or whom we refer to as "Nana" would do the same. My mom and dad never married and separated around my second birthday. Mom stayed in the back room in Nana's apartment and had this obsession with drinking Pepsi. She drank it like she drank water.

Dad had gotten full custody when I was around

three and it probably was for the best for everyone. My mom was just young. My mother's parents trusted my dad more than my mother when it came to raising me, so they helped him get custody.

Dad lived in West Oak Lane in an apartment and was newly married. In the year of 1978, I remember Dad taking me to his grandmother's home in Mantua section of Philadelphia. While there, his mother (my grandmother) took me to the store with her. I kept bugging her for a 10-cent water gun until she bought it.

Once we got back to the house, Grandpa hollered at her for getting it. I was too young to understand why but she snatched it away from me. At the store, I remember her telling me, "Don't show it to your grandfather" for some odd reason.

———

A year later, our family moved us to Fern Rock. I made a few friends and was allowed to play in the street with the older kids.

One afternoon, I got into big trouble. The older kids were playing football in the street when I grabbed the football and threw it, hitting a neighbor's window. I ran in the house while the boys were yelling, "Oooo, Oooo, Eric did it."

An older woman came a few minutes later and Mom-Bev called me downstairs. I was hiding upstairs beforehand. Mom-Bev asked, "Did you break this woman's window?"

"Yes, mom."

"How are you going to pay her back?"

"I don't know."

"Bring your piggy bank downstairs."

After a week, I got it back and got into trouble again, this time because of my cousin, D. He came, scheming on my money in the bank. "Yo, E, open it up," he kept pressing and I gave in. When Mom-Bev found out, she was pissed. About two years ago after releasing this book, I told her who made me do it and she was shocked.

In the summer of 1979, my aunt Kay (Mom-Bev's sister) took me to the movies around the corner to see "Alien." The movie attendants let us inside and it was one of the scariest flicks ever. I had nightmares about it especially the part when the Alien came out of the man's chest while he was eating.

Actually, I had some crazy nightmares at that age. Most were from watching the show 'Buck Rogers.' I'd hide behind the sofa whenever the aliens would appear. The good robot, Tiki, used to make this Beedi-beedi-bee sounds which irked the hell out of me. The female enemies fighting Buck Rodgers wore weaves you'll see in the hood nowadays. What a coincidence!

Since I was the only child back then, I'd hang out with the little girls around the way. They'd come by to take me out. Whenever my shoes became untied, there was a girl who would tie them for me when I pointed. After a few times, she showed me how to tie the and told me it was the last time she'd do it.

One evening during the late summer, Aunt Kay and I were walking past an alley where some Doberman Pinschers were on the loose. We made it back safely and I was out of breath and wheezing.

Having asthma and eczema almost stopped me from having a normal childhood. Mom-Bev made sure I wasn't overdoing things often checking in with me to see if I was relaxed. My eczema was so serious Mom-Bev would put hydrocortisone on and wrap me in plastic before bed to stop me from itching. For my asthma troubles, my parents got me a humidifier.

Then came the day when I played with matches and almost burnt the house down. I was lighting up pillows and putting them inside the washer, thinking I could turn it on to put out the fires. When Mom-Bev heard the smoke alarm go off, I got spanked.

Later that summer right before kindergarten, Mom-Bev put me in daycare and a worker would always put me in the corner. Mom-Bev got pissed and asked why I was being profiled. Maybe I was turning into a knucklehead.

———

Kindergarten for me wasn't pretty. One day after school, the bus driver dropped me off at the wrong house. My neighbors were out looking for me, believing something bad had happened. Somehow, I got home safely after someone saw me wandering around. They took me to the police station. In the late 70s – early 80s as you know, there was an epidemic of missing children's' cases. You'll find their pictures on milk cartons. It was a reminder every morning when you had your bowl of cereal.

After my kindergarten year finished, Dad purchased a house in Nicetown. The year was 1981 and I had one sister and another on the way, Mom-Bev and Dad deemed it was time for me to have my own room. Downstairs on the only color TV in the house, we had cable. HBO, Prism, and Showtime back then came with a special cable box with a large dial in the middle. Despite having cable, Dad often cut it on and off, complaining about the bill.

Lil E (that's me), the young boa (youngster in Philly dialect), loved him some VH1. Rod Stewart, Donna Summer, Lionel Richie, Michael Jackson, Cyndi Lauper, El-DeBarge, and other 80's pop stars' videos would be playing 24 hours a day. That was downstairs. In my room, there was a black-and-white 13" with an antenna you had to fix to make the stations clear.

Within a few months of settling in the new house, Mom-Bev began running an in-house daycare. Before I started 1st grade, I was her helper and sure enough, I didn't want that title. The best times of the day were the mornings when Dad used to leave bacon, scrapple, sausages, and eggs on the stove after he left for work. I tried being the first downstairs to grab some.

———

School is now in session and Steele School was my new second home. It was a fifteen-minute walk from my house and I'd stop off at the candy store along the way. There were two in that part of Nicetown at the time and my favorite was the one that sold one-cent cookies and candy. An old white woman owned one and would count our money exactly and give us that amount in return. No kidding! She'd count it right in front of you; not caring about the others in line who wished she'd hurry up.

Most of the youngsters at school spent their lunch money on candy in the morning and regretted it later. Some would beg you to share your lunch with them because they didn't have none. For those who were less fortunate, we ate the school lunches and most of us hated them. Just give me some candy, but that got me in big trouble one day.

Mom-Bev left some change under the phone in her bedroom and I noticing coins stacking up. I took a few every day and hoped she didn't notice. I went to the black-owned candy store one morning and the lady who ran it said, "Hey young man, where'd you get all this money from?" I told her my mom gave it to me. She asked for my phone number and I gave it to her like a dickhead. She then said she'd hold some of the candy until she talked to my parents or something like that. At first period, my teacher saw me chewing. "What do you got there, Mr. Eric?" I showed her my bag of candy, and she took it away.

When I got home later that day, it was all over for me. "Mom, I'm home." Mom-Bev came down staring at me. "Go to your room. Your dad will deal with you when he gets in."

"What did I do?"

"You know what you did. Go to your room."

It felt like forever before Dad came home. Once he did, my ass was in pain.

"No, no, please!" I screamed as Dad hit me with his brown leather belt.

After the whipping, I was put on punishment for a week; no TV, fun, and goodies. I was told to come straight home, do your homework, eat dinner, and go straight to bed.

THE CHEESE BUS

CHAPTER TWO

The first year at Steele made my parents cringe. They raised me the opposite of what they were experiencing. Sadly, the hood's impact is stronger in inner-city schools. Mom-Bev told her friends she couldn't have me acting like a damn criminal. My parents decided they'd had enough and changed my school.

In September 1981, I was on the yellow school bus aka "the cheese bus." The School District of Philadelphia's desegregation program went citywide and some of us took advantage of it. Before, residents of color had been demanding to send their kids outside for better education, but the racial divide and long trip to Northeast Philadelphia were the biggest barriers. Northeast was the last area to allow people like myself to come study. Townhall meetings were held for decades as residents voiced displeasure to the measure. You can look online under a document entitled: Philadelphia Desegregation, to view its full history including meeting notes.

How I found out about the process was from a green application with the word 'DESEGREGATION' written on top lying on the dining room table one afternoon. Clearly, at the age of seven, I didn't know what that meant.

The residents in Northeast Philadelpha at that time were predominately Irish. You'd rarely see a person of color up there out of fear of being attacked or perhaps killed. That area's town council would come up with all kinds of excuses on why students shouldn't be bused up there from other parts of the city. In the end, we got in.

———

Being at the new school felt different. However, I made friends regardless of color and learned sportsmanship through our extracurricular activities and gym class. Our gym teacher made the subject fun and it was by far the best time while we were at school. We played games like duck-duck-goose, kickball, dodgeball and others. If we had gym outside, we'd played lacrosse, softball, basketball and field hockey. There were times when we had track and field, too.

As the school year progressed, I learned how to play the violin, although I preferred the wind instruments. Since I was asthmatic, it was hard for me to blow out air. The day I auditioned for playing the trumpet, I sucked. In the afternoons when I got home, I'd go to my room to practice. In third grade, I was accepted into the school's orchestra which made my parents happy.

Outside of being good students, the kids fooled around when schoolteachers weren't paying attention; pushing one another when it was time to line up. The kids would slap one another in the back of the neck and buss (call each other bad names) throughout the day without curse words. Since I was one of the tallest, kids would single me out. If there was pushing in line, I got blamed. "It wasn't me," I countered but wasn't believed.

Mom-Bev delivered my second sister who was a bit fussy at times and Mom-Bev let me put her to sleep. My older sister and I would quarrel over who'd hold her, and since I was the oldest, it was a no-brainer.

My family lived in a lower-middle-class neighborhood in the upper North section of the city but not far from North Philadelphia. Both of my parents were working, and most of my neighbors were as well. We didn't have the same plights as our counterparts in the lower half of the city. As part of my role in the house, I was given trash duty on Wednesdays, and chores on Saturdays. Oftentimes I had to be reminded, but they got done.

———

I finished second grade on a strong note but didn't make the honor roll. By third grade, I did much better. We learned how to write cursive, and did a lot of spelling. My teacher, Ms. Carol kidded around but gave us plenty of homework. Before we entered her classroom, she'd straighten us out in line. "Get on the wall." If you clowned around, she'd call your house. By the time the third grade was over, I had made honor roll once.

In the fourth grade, things were a bit lax. Ms. Vicky was my homeroom teacher, who was in her mid to late thirties. I overheard some male teachers trying to go out with her but I don't think it ever happened. At lunch, she'd do cool activities for the students like host breakdancing and rap contests and other art stuff.

In her class, I met my close friends: James, Dan, and Rog. We were the tallest boys perhaps in the school besides a guy named Derrick who was in a grade higher. James and Rog used to make goofy sounds in the back of class whenever the teacher turned around. "Nightmare on Elm Street" had just come out, and Freddy Krueger was everyone's mind. Jazzy Jeff and Fresh Prince had a song about it and I was tired of hearing hour after hour on Power 99. That joint was straight whack.

———

Later that school year, I got in big trouble for being bringing fireworks to school. I bought them at a neighborhood store and told a few of my friends that day. At lunch, someone snitched. The disciplinarian, Ms. Mac, came looking for me around the school at lunchtime. She always looked serious and would suspend your ass in a heartbeat. Once she caught up with me, she pulled me to the closet in our homeroom. After opening my bookbag, she said, "Follow me to my office." I got suspended for three days.

This was my first suspension and I felt on my behind—literally. Dad put that leather on me so hard that night. While I was home, I stayed with Mom-Bev at her new daycare center on Germantown Avenue. I brought my Walkman along to listen to some rap songs and kept rewinding "Follow the Leader" to write down the lyrics in my notebook. Mom-Bev was pissed off but let me do my thing.

Mom-Bev knew the daycare's ins and outs, and others interested used to come by and consult with her throughout the day. Sometimes, parents brought their kids around my age to stay until they got off work free of charge. I remember this one girl (same age as me) came one afternoon when schools had a half-a-day city-wide. The young girl wanted to get her freak on, and I was afraid. She told me to look at her as she took off her clothes. I closed my eyes and she was pissed sighing. A few years later, I saw her all grown up, around the way looking good. "Man, I could have hit that," I kept telling myself.

Now that I was into rap music so much, I began buying blank tapes from the Chinese store around the corner. I'd record the mixes on Power 99 and often trade tapes with my friends Ev and Rob, on the block. If we weren't listening to music, we were playing with GIJoes, Transformers, Gobots, and Masters of Universe action figures.

———

The kids around the way including myself would rush home to catch the afternoon cartoons. Sometimes, I even skipped - *dont laugh.* Speed Racer came on at 2:00 PM and Gobots followed after at 2:30. I was able to catch the tail-end of Masters of the Universe and was in front of the screen to see GI Joe and Transformers on Channel 17 or 29 in their entirety.

Sometimes in the early evenings, Mom-Bev would have neighbors and friends from the neighborhood come by. I made friends with a boy name Kea by his mom and mine attending ceramics class. Dude was good at video games and I begged my parents to buy me a Commodore Vic-20 because he had one. I got bored with it fairly quickly. Mom-Bev later got me the Atari 2600, although 5200 and 7800 had best games. Aunt Sal had the 5200 but rarely let us play it when our family came over.

Around 1985-86, the Apple Macintoshes with the huge floppy 3-½ inch disk drives was the hottest computers on the market. Mayfair, my school, had bought a classroomful and our teacher shouted always at the end of class, "Don't forget your floppy disks." Some of us did anyway. We were taught LOGO (a graphics computer program from the 80s) which was pretty cool.

In the middle of the year, I joined the school's coin club headed by Ms. Robinson, our fourth-grade teacher. When she left her position, we all were sad to see her go.

I had a dislike for Art and Music class and didn't see why it was necessary. English sucked as well. Later in my thirties, I unintentionally became an English teacher while studying overseas to earn a living and sure enough, the money didn't suck.

When the weather broke, I'd go skateboarding and bike riding around Nicetown with my homies. Our block was different than the rest. From 20th and Wingohocking on down to 15th Street, everyone had their own way of being neighborly. Most of our parents told us to stay on the block and sometimes we disobeyed them. There were too many missing children cases that were unsolved back then. My block, Carlisle Street, was like one big family even though I didn't get along with most of the boys. For some reason, the older ones used to pick on me. I remember a time when my parents forced me to go out and fight. There were four boys; all older than me, and somehow, I fought every last one of them in front of the block. Every time I looked toward the house, Mom-Bev and Dad would signal for me to stay right there and fight. The moral of the story was *to never give up.*

When there was harmony, we play games like Truth, Dare, Consequence, and Repeat in the evenings with one another while our parents were inside. This was our first ways of getting our freak on. Nobody had sex but let's just say we saw some things.

———

Mom-Bev's grandmother gave me my first bike, a 'BMX', but it was a lemon. I had so many cuts and bruises from falling that I was thrilled when it finally broke down. My friends were riding around on the best bikes, popping wheelies and shit while I could only ride normally. I only should have been grateful for what I had.

Some boys around the way never went to school. Around Steele Elementary, they'd hang out looking for trouble. A boy with buck teeth that I had run-ins with was my main menace. Yet, crazily we became cool as shit in my teens.

———

For the summer break of 1984, my parents paid for me to go to overnight camp in Downingtown, PA for two weeks. I made two new friends; Milt and JP who were from neighborhoods right outside of Nicetown. There were five boys in our cabin including one funny white kid. A boy named Ernie happened to be the clown of the cabin. He'd get care packages almost daily. His parents must have loved him a lot because most of us didn't get shit in the mail. In the mornings before activities, the camp counselors would call out names for mail and mine wasn't called except once. There was no feeling like receiving a package from your folks even to this day. It made you feel good.

In the late mornings, we went camping, hiking, and did a few outdoor recreations. There were a few young girls who caught my eye, but the female lifeguards were the best. JP always had something to say about who looked good amongst the jawns ('girls' in Philly slang). When camp came was over, JP and I stayed in touch.

———

Back home, my dad was acting like an OG, cracking beers on the solo after work and sitting on the porch, watching the kids play. On the weekends, he'd hang out with his school buddies from West Philly who'd we call our uncles. They'd be down in Dad's basement like in a bunker in Vietnam with a red light on. When Dad was out at work or with his friends, I'd sneak down there and listen to his tapes seeing why the hell he was so into rock music.

From those of my Dad's friends who came by, Uncle Lonzo was the most frequent. During the holidays, he'd give all of us presents. I always hoped he didn't show up when I was in the doghouse. My family literally had a doghouse right above the stove and I was in. Sometimes, Dad would be in there when my mom was pissed off. Lying, stealing, and misbehaving were the mains reasons why I was in there.

When I was nine, Mom-Bev decided it was time to give me chores. One Saturday, she called me to her room and told me to bring whatever I was wearing for the week.

"I'm going to show you how to iron and you'll do it for yourself from now on," she said. "Do it now, so you won't have to do it later, son."

"Ok, mom."

"Also, you are now responsible for putting out the trash and recycle bins every Wednesday. And by the way, make sure you feed Penny in the morning before you go to school."

"Yes, Mom."

As I was learning the ropes of responsibility, I found my neighbor's grandson, Carlisle, in the same predicament. We'd hook up during the weekends and sometimes at night and play video games. I always wondered if he was named after our street name. Dude was one of the coolest friends ever. After graduating from Temple and breaking into acting, he suddenly passed away from asthma. *My man for life!*

Another friend of mine on the block named Evey used to talk shit whenever we played sports on Nintendo especially Tecmo Bowl. He had the best team (1985 Chicago Bears) with Walter Payton and Mike Singletary and they were unstoppable. I'd play with the Colts or the Dolphins and it was hard to win. If we got bored with Tecmo Bowl, we'd play Double Dribble where the win-loss ratio was more in my favor (he'll dispute this). Whenever I was over his crib, his family treated me like their son and I am forever grateful. Big ups to those who are living and have passed on.

———

One girl a few houses away from Evey on the opposite

side of the street name 'Ace' used to get on my nerves. I had to stay at her house whenever Mom-Bev wasn't home in the afternoons. When I came, I'd find her grandma, Ms. Lynn, watching the Oprah Winfrey Show. If I ask, "Can I watch cartoons, Ms. Lynn?"

"No."

While when my sisters, Ace and I were coming home from school, I'd chase them home and it was amusing. Always loved me some Ms. Lynn, Aunt Jerry, and Ms. Pat.

———

Back in my days, girls would be around the way wearing spandex and big ass gold earrings even at school. New students started attending Mayfair from West Philly, Mount Airy, and West Oak Lane when I was in the fifth grade. This girl from out Westside used to wear the tightest jeans in school and those curves were major. I hate to be blunt but we were in the fifth grade and she could have passed for an eighteen-year-old. Even our gym teacher tried hitting on her and got fired. He tried getting the girl in his office on the creep and got dimed on. Everybody was like "Damn," when his ass got caught. I can't remember he got fired.

At lunchtime, the boys would beatbox, break-dance, rap, and play sports. The youngins in my generation wore two-tone Lees, Air Jordans, Adidas sweatsuits and anything fashionable around the way. Unfortunately, I was the exception. My next-door-neighbor had these joints from Payless called Eagles which were replicas of Air Jordans. I had even worse.

In 1985, Run DMC, LL Cool J, and the Fat Boys were the hottest hip hop artists out in my opinion. "Krush Groove" the movie had come out and put hip-hop on the map. Schoolly D (the first gangsta rapper), and MC Breeze were representing Philly along with Lady B from Power 99 who happened the first female MC of Hip Hop.

The New York hip-hop scene had Philly beat by a long shot; Africa Bambaataa, Grandmaster Flash, and the Furious Five, Scorpio, Kurtis Blow, Kool Moe Dee, Run-DMC, LL Cool J, and the Fat Boys were leading the genre. The Sugar Hill Gang's, "Rapper's Delight" was still the shit even though it was released in 1979.

Rap music back then had mainly positive messages such as staying off drugs, black consciousness, and upliftment. (Read my book series: The History of Hip Hop to learn more)

East Coast rap music was all about the lyrics despite being in an era of so much negativity in the Black community worldwide. The crack epidemic, droughts in Africa, AIDS, prostitution, missing children, wars, cannibalism, and corruption were the main headlines on every news station. Between the political bigots and even our own parents, Hip-Hop was labeled as criminal. It wasn't until around the late 1980s and maybe the early 1990s when the public's opinion changed. The rise of Hip-Hop took the world by surprise making it the greatest form of urban art & expression.

———

Mom-Bev began sending me to church rather than staying at home doing nothing on Sunday mornings. Before leaving, I'd be up around 6 AM to see "Feed the Children" on TV. The pictures of malnourished babies in Ethiopia were so shocking. The show had their cameras constantly on children with flies on their faces having these potbellies. I hate to admit but I felt that ministries deliberately twisted the narrative by going to the villages and filming in the rural areas where things are a bit more underdeveloped. I learn about these ministries while traveling through

Africa. *Don't let the cameras fool you. Africa is blessed.*

Mom-Bev would dress me in a suit and tie and wipe the crust off my face before leaving. I never watched my face correctly. I went alone while my friends on the block were still sleeping. Church was straight-up boring. I'd fall asleep, while the people sang. I just couldn't get into it because it was too early in the damn day. A few years later in my teens, my Sunday school teacher was walking around the hood shouting at the devil with her hair all fanned out. I think she was suffering from mental illness.

One Sunday after service, I came home and told my Dad while he was taking off my tie, I wanted to be a Muslim. *I don't know where that came from? I never even heard of a Muslim.*

"Son, it's your decision when you get old enough." Dad wasn't the churchgoing type and Mom-Bev was the opposite. I don't remember anyone going on Sunday nights, especially the kids I knew.

On holidays, we would visit my dad's parents home in West Philly. Grandma always had the best graham crackers and cooked the best cornbread. Grandpa

Reese would sit in the room joking with us and always put a smile on your face. When he died, we lost a good man.

My cousins were funny; making noises no one knew except themselves. My oldest cousin fell in love with a guy named Darnell back then but unfortunately, she's still single.

———

During fifth grade, my classes in school got a bit harder. Ms. Carmen, our homeroom teacher, would make us do everything although she was a nice teacher. Some classmates' parents came up to the school and kicked their asses sometimes in front of the class for horsing around. "Don't make me come up there and whip yo ass boy. Let me hear one more time, you acting up. I sent you to school to learn not to act like a fool," was often mentioned by our parents back in the day. Thank God for good parenting!

Back then, our schools didn't have metal detectors. We only had school security known as NTAs. Most were older black women and for the most part, we treated them respectfully because they were the same ages as our mothers. The NTAs were also in charge of the school buses before and after school. Ms. Watson was my assigned NTA and she had this drippy Jeri-Curl. She'd yell, "Be quiet or I'll write you all up." Sadly, the NTAs had the longest work days and received peanuts in exchange.

———

That year, Mom-Bev shut down the daycare on Germantown Avenue because it wasn't making money and got a job working at a bank in Center City. Her clients were sad, but Mom-Bev felt it was time to move on.

In the mid-80s, everyone had a silver or gold belt with their name on it. I got a silver-one for my birthday, I believe. It was the era of Adidas sweatsuits, stopwatches, pagers, high and low top fades, Jeri-Curls, Jeffs and Shags which were all black hairstyles back in that were in. For Easter, when the neighborhood gets dressed up, I wore my first Adidas sweatsuit purchased from Erie Avenue. Fashion brands like Sergio Tacchini, MCM, PB, and Fila were in and two-tone Lee jeans were still, too.

A boy from school named Gee from around the way started being my nemesis. We had this on-again and off-again friendship and it was weird. Our mothers became cool because we fought so much. If there was harmony between us, we'd be cracking jokes on the school bus and sometimes that'll break our truce. Whoever came up with the silliest jokes, got mad props. At night, I'd be in my bedroom, practicing for the next day.

The crack epidemic reached our hood and several of our neighbors started freebasing. The hood deemed them as smokers, baseheads, or crackheads. Some died, and some got it together.

————

Run-DMC came to the Spectrum (used to be our hometown stadium) in July or August 1985 for the 'My Adidas' tour and I straight up missed it. My play uncle Lonnie said he got me tickets but didn't come through when he found out I was acting up around the house.

Then in the early fall, the bombing on the MOVE members in Southwest Philadelphia shook up our city. It was the most devastating event in our city's history. Then-mayor Wilson Goode Sr. either gave or oversaw (depends on who you ask) the go-ahead to drop a bomb on a house in the middle of a residential neighborhood. That bomb brought down at least two blocks of houses and killed nine people, including women and children. The mayor still hasn't formally apologized and recently was endorsed to have a block in West Philly named after him. *Hell no!* Two people of the MOVE house survived; Ramona and Birdee Africa, the latter being a child or toddler. Both got paid a few million dollars from the city and Ramona nowadays is ailing. Peace and Love!

A PHILLY ADOLESCENCE

CHAPTER THREE

Alas, the summer of 1988 and it was a scorcher. Those days were the hottest in Philly's history with a streak of forty consecutive days of ninety-degree weather. The nights were worse with the humidity and everyone and their grandma was outside cooling off before bedtime. On top of that, our city's Trash Department went on strike. The smell of trash around Wayne Junction was nauseating and maggots and all types of rodents were around. Residents from Nicetown and Brickyard took their trash and dumped it under the bridges at Wayne Junction. We did the same. During the strike, I got my first job stocking goods at Aunt Jackie's (a family friend) convenient store on Wayne & Pulaski Avenue. Most days I had to take the long way to get to work because of the trash dumps under both bridges.

In 1988, there were crackheads galore and hoes up on every corner giving up pussy (I hate to be so frank). Pimps in Cadillacs and Rolls Royces were picking them up and the oldheads were tricking. There were also maniacs roaming around killing everybody. You'd see on Action News that this body was found butchered and then minutes later, another. When the commercials came on, there was a surplus of anti-drug campaigns and even on billboards across town. Remember the commercial, "It will make you feel good, good, good..." Then, it would end with a young person saying, "Just say no." Ministers were on Sunday mornings were preaching nonstop while nonprofits were hauling in donations. It was a time of total chaos and mass confusion.

However, between 1988 and 1989, hip hop took off. Big Daddy Kane, the Juice Crew, KRS-One, Eric B & Rakim, Public Enemy, LL Cool J, Ultramagnetic MCs, EPMD, Run DMC, The D.O.C., NWA and many more exploded onto the scene. New Kids on the Block, Boyz to Men, and Bobby Brown who went solo put out their debut albums. Roxanne Shante and The Real Roxanne had a rap battle going on; provoking Shante to destroy the other's rap career forever. Next, there were Philly rap artists; Steady B and Cool C from the Hilltop Hustlers, Tuff Crew, 3x Dope along with Jazzy Jeff and Fresh Prince who represented. Our parents were into Keith Sweat, Anita Baker, Luther Vandross, Teddy Pendergrass, Michael & Janet Jackson along with Sade and Atlantic Starr who were the leading R&B artists out. In the evenings, Tony Brown, radio host for the show called the Quietstorm, would play what we called "baby-making music" at 10 PM.

Yet, the hustlers who were rocking gold chains, flashing beepers, and talking about their posse had a major influence on the hoods and kids tried their best to copy them. "What posse you from, homes?" The term "posse" was in and everyone was using it. The Jamaicans had candy shops fronting as weed spots and you can spot them a mile away wearing those crazy-looking Paco jeans. The Ricans wore them, too. It was craziness in the hood, believe me when I tell you.

My eighth-grade year was going quite smoothly until Christmas night. That's when I got jumped. It was a Black damn Christmas! I was walking with a friend to go play some video games around 7 PM. My relatives were over, watching football and enjoying the holiday.

There's a parking lot that crosses from my street to my friend's and while we were walking, a group of boys jumped me. My friend didn't even help me out. He stood there and watched because he was cool with them. I ran home and wept; banging on the walls in my room. Mom-Bev came running upstairs and comforted me. I was losing the hardihood, and suicide had crossed my mind. I felt like an attraction for anyone looking to get their shit off. Still, I believed that brighter days were coming.

———

Three months later, I caught the chickenpox and was out for close to two weeks and missed my final exam for Wood Shop. Gladly, high schools determined your eligibility from your last report card in seventh and first in the eighth. My parents didn't want me any local schools, so my school counselor helped me apply to a few including Central High. Central was considered the top academic school in the city.

Graduation day was nearing and Mom-Bev took me down Third and Market to pick out a graduation suit. I got a white one and it was fly.

Since the weather was breaking, there were several

intermural track meets and our school was part of them. My track squad came in second because the guy after me fumbled the baton. He blamed me, but it was his fault.

During the week of the meet, I got into trouble on the cheese bus. The kids including me were acting up because the NTA was out that day. We threw crayons at the bus driver as he drove and everyone on the back of the bus was suspended from riding the bus for a week. My parents were upset but I didn't get a beating. Still, Dad and Mom complained to relatives and friends about me and I hated it.

When I got back to school, I put one of my friends down with 2 Live Crew's album, "Move Something" and he got in trouble because his parents heard him listening to it. Once a month, I'd go to his house to play Sega Genesis and his dad was really strict, always checking me out whenever I was over. He might have been getting money on the down low. As you know in the hood, the game doesn't have an age limit.

Finally, I got good news in the mail that I was accepted in Central High School. "Hard work pays off, son", Dad kept repeating as Mom-Bev told everyone and I mean everyone. Nevertheless, my issues with the neighborhood bullies continued and they would chase me from Buy-Rite supermarket all the way to my doorstep every time they spotted me. It's was almost time for me to stand up!

Good lord! It's graduation day, June 17th, 1989; the date of the real commencement of Eric Reese.

E THE PENPAL?

CHAPTER FOUR

All the drama you've read so far makes you wonder whether or not I ever had a girlfriend. This chapter will set the record straight, so sit back and enjoy.

The summer of 1989 was almost worse than '88. The Trash Department went on strike again and the hood was stinking. Old folks and young were vexed. An Italian guy, Paulie, and his brother who owned Buy-Rite on Broad and Wingohocking hired a bunch of people from the neighborhood to work as cashiers, stock persons, security and butchers. The kids worked also as baggers and most were between the ages of ten and sixteen. You could earn 25 to 40 dollars a day bagging up people's groceries easily. Come before the market opened at 8 AM or reserve a spot with your cashier the night before. If not, you'll be ass out. Sometimes, young boys & girls around the way got to the market as early as 7:15. With the money earned, I was on my way to getting myself some fresh gear. I was tired of not wearing no-name stuff. I wanted to look good, have a girlfriend and chill. Now that school is out, it was grinding season.

If I couldn't get a spot bagging at the market, my friend Kea and I went down the Gallery in Center City. This guy just kept repeating the word "bitties" one day and I got hooked. The meaning of bitties according to him was "girls" and he was the first nigga I heard use the term. "Look at those bitties, man. Go talk to that bitty, E." Kea kept pushing to get the ladies' phone numbers. One weekend, Kea lost all of his money with those fake-ass gambling jokers known in our town. They set up boxes and get you to play three-card monte and they'll let you win the first time on purpose just to get you to gamble more. You'd lose in the end and that's what happened to Kea. I told him not to but he didn't listen. The shit was crazy!

———

The common phrase, "As long as you got clothes on yo back, we did our job," wasn't hitting for me. Despite it being true, it does not check out well with growing up being black. Being "black" means you have to look good in all retrospects.

Kea would invite me to his church on Sundays, and it was the golden opportunity to check out the bitties. As the preacher gave his sermon, we were checking them out. On Saturday mornings, we'd go jogging at LaSalle and finish our course inside an hour. We started this doing the cold months which were the hardest. Kea would jog in these blue Fila sneaker boots and the scene was funny.

We took a few weekends off from going downtown and the next time, we did it was a bit more positive. There was a group of African American travelers coming out of the Gallery and walking in our direction. Among them, was a gorgeous dark-skinned girl. The girl kept looking at me as we walked past. Kea was like, "E, get her number. She's on you, man." I stopped them and started up a conversation. "Hi, I see you're not from here. Are you?"

"No, we're from South Carolina. Philly is nice!" the young girl or her mother said.

Kea was chatting with the mother and aunt while I

centered in on the girl. "Hey, by the way. Can I get your phone number? I wanna talk to you later."

"Sure." She wrote down two numbers and then told me she was staying at the hotel nearby.

"Bet. I'll call you later, so we can hook up. Nice to meet you all," I said walking away.

Kea was like, "E, you bold, man. You did that right in front of her peoples."

"Yes, sir."

———

Later that evening, I called the girl and she told me that her mom and aunt was with her when we met earlier. She went on to tell me that they were leaving Philly tomorrow to fly to Ohio to see some relatives. I told her I hoped to see her before she heads out. The girl then told me to come to the hotel around midnight and give her a call and she'll let me in. She gave me the name of the hotel, and I waited until close to 11 PM to sneak out the house. I didn't call her before coming. What a mistake! Once I got there, I told the receptionist her name, but he said no one under that name was checked in. I kept calling the number she gave me on the payphone outside but she didn't pick up. Maybe the girl was playing games?

A few days later, the girl called me to clear up things insisting she was up waiting on me but fell asleep. "Yeah. Yeah." I was salty but we kept in touch by writing letters and shit and she even mailed me photos of her. I long-distance called her from the house phone and my parents were pissed about the bill. I discovered my first love. "Write letters only, son," Mom-Bev repeated. "Yeah, Yeah." If I was out, I'd even try calling from a friend's or neighbor's house. I just couldn't keep that girl off my mind.

Kea told me I was crazy. "How are you even in a relationship and y'all don't live in the same city?"

After a month or so, the girl started saying she loved me. My sisters would tease me. "Eric got a girl-friend." My parents got the long-distance calling shut off and it was messed up.

Around the same time, I also met a cheerleader from Camden down the Gallery. She was going down the escalator and I was going up. "Shorty! Let me holler at you for a minute," I yelled. She had one of the most gorgeous smiles I'd ever seen and her body was fit. We tried writing for a while, but we were close enough to see each other. I'd take the Patco train to Camden and hit up her crib on Wildwood Avenue. The girl had a pink room and I was falling for her. We kissed and all but nothing went down. Not sure what happened to us, but hopefully we'll see each again. *LOL, Neva!*

I was growing up and some of my boys called me "the out-of-state playa." Girls from Philly were getting on my nerves and out-of-state girls just seemed to be easier and more open-minded. On route with Kea, I had joints from Jersey, Virginia, Maryland, DC, and other parts of PA on my radar. My phone book was getting fat; all filled with girls numbers. Anyway, that lasted for a hot minute, so you'll have to read Book Two to find out what happened next.

THERE AND NOW

VOLUME TWO

FOREWORD

"If you're scared to take chances, you'll never have
the answers." – Nas

WELCOME TO HIGH SCHOOL

CHAPTER FIVE

After eighth grade graduation, I started working under a summer program called Phil-A-Job. It was a city-funded work program for youths to keep them off the streets during the summer. They placed me at the Lingual Institute in Center City. The CEO showed me the ins and outs of office work and I was given data entry assignments along with answering phones. Every Friday, he would give a 25-cent raise. We were working for minimum wage back then which was $3.75 an hour. By the program's end, I was making close to $6.00 an hour. The CEO commended me throughout my time there and wished me the best.

The summer of 1989 passed by with no major drama. Still, my parents weren't budging about getting me any fly clothes yet. Once my freshman year began, I was wearing a pair of Pro Wings. My first day, I was looking like a Kmart fashion model. First period began and I had Biology. Luckily, I was sitting next to the best-looking girl in school who was from South Philly. The girl was red-boned and had rose-looking hair.

I had to get fly if I wanted a chance. Yet, that was hard because even to get a haircut from the local barber was an issue with my peoples. "Go down your cousin's house (in West Philly). He'll cut it for free." That's what I was told.

The red-bone and I were lab partners and I tried spitting game her way, but she had a man. She did tell me if she was single, she'd give me the time and day. And that was all I needed to hear. As I began settling in school, I swung my attention to this slim brown-skin shorty. She'd want me to kiss her on the staircase next to the cafeteria when nobody was around. I can't remember her name but she was so short I had to stoop down whenever I did. I guess it was just a school fling.

The worst subjects at school were Typing and Pascal. Typing was so freaking boring and Pascal was for weirdos. I met my man Pee from the Westside in one of the two. We fooled around in the hallways while we changing classes and chatted about hip hop, DJing, and girls at school.

After school, I headed to the JV football tryouts. I

worked out for being the team's punter but couldn't make the cut. Then, I tried out for the track squad but didn't make it either. My mind was on love and hip hop.

My peers secretly betted on football games on Mondays. The white boys had the pools and went around the school hustling. I tried it a few times and lost but nothing significant. Our school was so diversified you'd think we were students of those who worked for the United Nations. For the most part, there were good vibes.

———

Close to the second semester, this girl named Kee from Mount Airy and I became real cool. Mount Airy girls were perceived back then as being conceited mainly because they were light-skinned and on a higher income level than most of us. Anyway, she was going out with this dude on the football team. We fell out over something one time and she told her boyfriend I disrespected her. That nigga said something I didn't appreciate, so I told my man JP (from the overnight camp in Downingtown).

My man used to hang around with a few of his homies cracking on chicks up Broad and Olney in the mornings. One morning, I'm standing up at Girls High with JP and his crew before school and Kee's boyfriend walked past us, staring. I gritted back telling JP that was Kee's boyfriend. Moments later, Kray got sucker-punched and ran away holding his face. I didn't know it was going to go down like that, but shit happens.

The dude didn't come up to school for a few days. Somehow, he and his crew caught me walking alone down Olney Avenue and jumped me. Negroes didn't really do nothing. I fought back but came away with a few dirt stains. I called JP and told him. It wasn't even worth it. Kee and Kray fell out a week later and she started wanting me. What a world!

Got a call a few evenings later from Kee asking me to cut school and come to her house. Yes, sir! She was bragging how she could beat me in Uno and all. I asked her about Kray and she said he wanted her back but she was good. The next day, I got to her crib around 9:30 in the morning. We played Uno for a few games and then things heated up. We went down to the basement and while one of her friends was on the phone with her, it was all she wrote.

———

It felt so strange. There was some mustiness, and you

know where I'm going with this. There was some movement upstairs causing us to pause. I hid in the bathroom leaving the rubber near the toilet. Kee thought her grandma was home, but it was the postman. I had to be at work around two, so I left out and didn't have time to shower. While sitting on the XH, I was smelling like fish. I just made to work on time. Once I clocked in, I went straight down to the cellar.

"I'll be in the basement doing inventory until you call me and please don't" were my thoughts.

"Eric, can you bring up some--?" the clerks upstairs kept calling me. No one said anything, but I know they smelled SEX on me. I told JP what happened when I got off and he busted out laughing. A few weeks later, I got fired for trying to add hours on my timecard. JP got the job after me and worked there for years.

At the end of school year, I failed two classes and had to go to freakin' summer school, man. However, I wanted to resume working with Phil-A-Job, so I went to Southern because it was within walking distance.

E GOT IN TROUBLE

This year in Phil-A-Job they put me in training at the Houston Rec Center from 12 to 4 in the afternoon. After the first few days, a brother named Pone and I meshed. We hung out at lunch and etc., realizing we had a lot in common. Pone was from down Passyunk projects at the bottom of the city. Whenever he talked, I saw wisdom from his street smarts. I felt like a student of this brother. The ladies at the gig wanted him although he didn't fall for them. Pone never took a man's word for face value. One of the realest ever.

We'd hit up liquor stores and hang out all over the city after class. Kool Keith, Baldin, Darryl, and others from the Southside joined us. These were my homies whom I met through Pone. We'd put up to get forty ounces of Old E, Colt 45, St. Ides, and Red Bull just like the oldheads around the way. There were times where Baldin would get Blue Bull for $1.45 but that shit was nasty. The crew was always taken care of and sometimes we'd take one straight to the head.

All of us were fourteen doing it like it should be done. If anybody from the squad earled (vomited), we'd made sure they got home safe. Tee from Passyunk who didn't drink or smoke was our partner as well. He was a couple years older than us and stayed geared up. Tee would be rockin' that Nautica with Porsche Design glasses. Once, he was heading to the exit of the Yunk (Passyunk Projects) while Pone and I were at Darryl's house hanging out. Tee sold us some weed and for the first time, my world was spinning. We were lit and our eyes were redder than Mars.

———

Up North, I starting rolling with some old heads up B and O (Broad and Olney) along with JP and his crew. It was all gravy. Jimmy was the head of the crew and was a cousin to my man Kea down Nicetown. Dude was down for whatever. When we rolled, we were eight to ten deep. We drank so much that we didn't care. From hopping the train, stealing candy out of Rite Aid or causing a ruckus, we'd be doing our thing.

Pretty boys would be frontin' (acting like they are down, but not) and the squad made them look silly. "Take that chain off, give up those sunglasses and hand over those beepers." "Hey girl, let me get your phone number." If the girls fronted, the reply simply was "Fuck you, bitch." *Yeah, it was raw back then but you'd understand if you were in the mix.* In Center City, we'd go to the arcades to hang out, but also to catch suckers slippin'.

———

After two-and-a-half weeks into my summer job stint, I got into trouble with the law for the first time. The story goes as the following:

The story goes as:

On a hot and humid night in July 1990, my crew went ballistic. We were intoxicated, walking down 8th and Spruce when two men passed by us holding hands. My boys were yelling and screaming and just beat them up for fun. I karate-kicked one at the end just following along. Afterward, we went to Walnut and Locust Train Station. As we entered, cops scrambled around looking for someone. Since we were so deep, their attention shifted on us. The group split up; some walking solo normally and others ran, like me. I ran across the tracks to the opposite platform and headed upstairs to the street level as if nothing happened. As I was walking away, a tall black in plain clothes yelled at me. I could have acted like nothing happened but I ran like a dummy. He ran and caught up with me at an alley off of 13th and Chestnut. He then tackled me and bashed my face in with his shoe.

"This is fucking police brutality man and I'm filing a report," I shouted.

His reply: "Go right ahead."

The cops arrived, cuffed me and took me with two of the crew already shackled inside the paddy wagon which felt like a pizza oven. We pleaded for air, but they didn't give a fuck.

Off to the Roundhouse on 8th and Vine, the paddy wagon kept hitting bumps. I vomited once they took us inside the police station. The cops and detectives on duty were giggling at their desks. "Fuck all of y'all," I thought as I passed by. My face was sandy from the imprints of that black cop's shoe. Three of us were taken to the same holding cell and made to wait for hours. Inside, we reflected on how the shit went down.

Two detectives came and took me out for finger-printing. They made you rub your hands with this black jelly to clean your fingers to take the prints. At the age of fourteen, I'm now a convict. From watching all of those movies, I knew I'd at least a phone call to make. Who would I call? Mom and Dad? I asked and was denied. After fingerprinting, the cops came back and gave us ice tea and cheese sandwiches. I only drank ice tea. The toilets in the joint were made of aluminum and I'm not taking any chances.

Forty-eight hours later, I was held at the Juvenile Justice Center (JJC) on 20th and Vine Street. Once inside, some boys were checking me out and then almost jumped me later in the day. The staff moved me to another floor before so. On the new floor, we watched movies all day and played board games. I remember seeing Bruce Li on one of the movies. As the day went on, it seemed like everyone had a story and mine was to just get the hell out.

The next morning, I was taken along with other juveniles to the basement in orange jumpsuits. Then we were transported to the court on Vine St. The judge would read aloud the charges against you via television monitor. I was sent to a home in Southwest Phil-adelphia for pretrial. For a month, while I was there, most of the juveniles treated the place like it was home. The counselors allowed us to watch movies, play basketball in the front, take walks, and etc. There was one guy who thought he was tough, so I avoided contact with him. One evening at curfew, when the lights went out, that guy and others locked the door and jumped me for no reason. I fought back and after-ward, it was said that it was an initiation.

The next day, I was transferred to another home in Yeadon, which turned out to be a roach motel. Turn on the light after 8 o'clock and you will see what I'm talking about. I even had to go to the emergency room because of my asthma. The boys at the home were crazy, but not literally. They would put matches between our toes and toothpaste under pillows at night. It happened to me once and the look on my face expressed that it will never happen again.

After a week at that place, I was again moved to another home in West Oak Lane. The lady there was stricter than your great-grandma. There were four boys there and she took us out to Cheltenham Mall once or twice a week. Her home was the best. I have to admit she treated us the best.

My court date came, and you know I was scared to

death. It was my first offense and there were multiple likelihoods. Around noon, the judge gave me a year of probation and restitution of ten dollars and an apology to the victims. I never apologized wholeheartedly but no I am. I'm truly sorry and hope one day, I'll see you both again. After the sentencing, I ran straight to Mom-Bev arms and sobbed. JP and Dad were there as well. When I asked to go to JP's house afterward, they let me go.

———

A week later, after settling in, I caught up with the squad up Broad and Olney. Niggas were glad to see me out but one of the homies was still down because he had an adult record. People around my way wondered how the young nerd got in trouble. A little hood respect was all I always asked. Since I missed so many days at summer school, I had to repeat the ninth grade at Central for two classes. It was confusing learning that I would be in a tenth-grade homeroom but have ninth grade status.

However, there were still a few weeks left at Phil-A-Job and the homies showed me love when I got back. I remember the day I came back I was wearing red and black Adidas with red sweats and a matching t-shirt. I was fresh, but couldn't drink or smoke. Pone filled me in on what I missed, who he smashed, and etc. A new guy, Ron, from the Bottom (Mantua), was there and began hanging out with us. He didn't smoke or drink but he pulled the ladies. I hung out around his way a few times and met this dark-skinned girl at one of his parties. She looked good and you know I was going for the gusto.

"E" THE MISFIT DJ

My first gig deejaying ended being a dud. Ron asked me to deejayed a party at his house once and my equipment broke down. Ronski brought in another from around the way and luckily, we had a good time that night. A few days later, the dark-skinned girl around Ron's way came to my house after school. I couldn't get "No skins" because my baby sister kept cockblocking. We were smooching in bed when she popped in saying, "Oooo, Eric. I'm telling Mommy." I made a deal with her not to tell but they found out anyway.

High school was in effect and if I didn't pass all my subjects, I'd be left down in the 10th grade instead of the 11th. I was checking everybody out on the low. There were a few Muslims who were the new freshmen and at first appeared to be cool. As the first month of school passed, I saw them as pretty boys frontin'.

Meanwhile, Pee (my 9th-grade partner) and I at lunch, squabbled about the best hip-hop artists. When the girls walked by, we'd be like "Daaaaaam". One caught our attention named Ali. She was in the 11th and rolled alone. Pee and I challenged each other to see who'd get her. Somehow, I caught her at lunch some days later and struck up a conversation. She gave me her number, and we hit it off. I kept our little thing on the low from Pee for over a week. Man was amazed when he saw us holding hands in the lunchroom. "I told you so, young boa."

After school, I ride home with my girl and walk her to the door like a gentleman. We would kiss and embrace up to her front porch. Lovebirds and yes, it was sensational. My girl didn't talk much, but her lips spelled the revolution.

Before I met Ali, I had a friend at school from Erie Avenue named Tavon. The ladies were on his left and right. My man had some good pickings. We'd play ball together for lunch and gossip after school. I think he was on my team the first time I dunked the basketball.

Suddenly, he stopped coming. We had a big history exam, and he didn't come. I asked our history teacher, Mr. Rob about my man's absence and he pulled me out right before the exam, telling me Tavon had drowned in the Schuylkill River about a week ago. I broke down and Mr. Rob embraced me asking if I wanted to delay the exam. I still took it wondering if some of my classmates already knew.

Tavon was my man and although I didn't meet his family, his memory still holds a place in my heart. After his passing, my difficulties at home got worse. Dad and I started fighting. He recently lost his job and began drinking heavily. I was going through my adolescence and it seemed like every little incident escalated into something bigger.

———

One evening, Dad and I got into a fight because I came home late and it turned into Clash of the Titans. I had cuts, bruises, and scratches all over. I went to school the next day looking like a freed prisoner of war.

My play uncle and aunt in East Mount Airy got me to come stay with them until things cooled off. Their neighborhood was so clean and quiet that you could leave your bike outside all night and no one would touch it. However, a neighbor yelled at me once when he assumed I stole his grandson's bike because I wasn't from around there. My play cousin told him it wasn't me and he apologized.

My cousin had this girlfriend that liked me but was too goofy to say something. I'd go by her house and chill in her bedroom but we were young back then. We did go to a few house parties together, but nothing happened between us.

Honestly, I didn't want to go back home. The atmosphere in Mount Airy is where I belonged. Yet, I went down the way whenever I could. My homies knew the deal but we had other things to catch up on. Sometimes, my play cousin came to the hood and the boys would sweat the shit out of her because she was redbone. My late buddy Richard Sawyer Jr. had the best chance at getting her. Crazily, they could have passed for brother and sister.

One afternoon after school, something unusual happened days after I learned of the death of my friend Tavon. I was solo in the kitchen, smoking a cigarette when something on the table moved. Then, the phone started ringing nonstop and a few things were moving around. I wasn't high! When I picked up the phone, I heard these eerie noises. It could have been Tavon reaching out. Nevertheless, it was the jinns playing with me.

My play cousin began going out with this guy who in high school was working two jobs. He was a manager for a shoe store up Cheltenham Mall and forgot the other. We hung out together a few times and dude was cool as shit. After a year or so, they broke up which was shocking.

———

My probation was coming to an end and I was glad. Now, I was back at the house and Pone and I would produce new rap songs at his house or mine. We put out so many rap songs with or without cursing that we might have had about five albums worth of content. Every time we got together, we put down a track. Our shit was tight and we held faith that we'd break into the industry one day. Philly was a hard spot to shine because of the New York market but we had it.

Pone and I were walking through my hood from Broad Street one night when we passed by a few of my childhood bullies. We shook our hands and for the first time, I had heart to speak. I told those niggas I'm older now and that old shit would cease. They were surprised to hear me not giving a fuck. However, they gave me my respect and from that time onward, I never had a problem with dem niggas ever again.

Being bullied was over. Lil E became E and Pone is my partner for life. There aren't many I've come across who could match that man's street smarts.

———

It's the summer of 1990 and I made a few friends up in another neighborhood not far from Nicetown called Hunting Park. We used to smoke blunts most of the day, listen to hip hop and cracked on (talked to) the girls. The group, Three Times Dope, and Tuff Crew were the hottest Philly groups out and they were from all around the way. Seeing Philly being put on the map, I started taking deejaying more seriously. Jam Master Jay, Jazzy Jeff, DJ Premier, DJ Scratch, and Terminator X were the deejays I tried emulating. They'd be killin' it. Whenever I heard their scratches, I found it so futuristic.

I saved some money and got a turntable set, not 1200s, but Technics. Pone and I sampled beats from everything and we put a lot of creativity in our mixes. The best rappers that were out were Rakim, Gangstarr, Kool G Rap, KRS-One, Public Enemy, Scarface, NWA, Geto Boys, and a lot of other underground

MCs. Basically, anyone who didn't sell their souls to radio stations was on our list. The way we rapped was hardcore but poetic. Pone was one of the best I've heard. His rhyming style was unmatched. We did a song "Mental Torture" which could have been a hit for the ages. The combination of sampling one of Kool G Rap joints and some eerie sounds made the beat dope. I co-rhymed, beat-made, and scratched, while Pone was the lead. It didn't matter if the beat was fast or slow, or we freestyled or wrote the rhymes down, we still killed it. People who knew of our rap talent gave us love, but we didn't have contacts to reach New York.

———

Back to school and eleventh grade was a breeze academically for me except for Geometry and Chemistry classes. Yet, a few sophomores started feeling themselves and you know I wasn't impressed. I'm glad my Chemistry teacher, Mr. Perry, was there to help me deal with some of my issues. He saw I was having difficulties, so he'd pull me to the side and advise me. Mr. Perry was like a father figure and his smile alone made you happy. You could talk to him about anything. All you had to do is find him.

Around the latter half of the school year, my man

Pone came up to Central and got into a fight with one of the sophomores. Before this, no one asked about others coming on school grounds. That day, Pone and I was chilling in the cafeteria when this dude started staring at us. Pone stepped to him and it was a rap. Nobody stepped in it from the other pretty boys because we'd have to all rumble. The fight barely lasted a minute. When school security came, we jetted and those bitch ass niggas snitched on us. Pone and I went up to his school which wasn't far away and school security there was on us from the jump. We got caught, or fled, I can't remember but when we got back to my house, the school called. We were smoking some bud out back when the phone rang. They asked to speak to the man or woman of the house. I pretended like I was my father speaking but they still called later in the evening. It was a crazy day from beginning to end.

———

Both schools were able to get in touch with our parents and we were suspended. The day I when I returned to school, everyone from that pretty-boy group was gritting (looking) on me. "Let's do this one-on-one because you are a group of pussies," I ranted whenever I saw them. Fuck what ya heard. Pone and I didn't need a crew to handle shit. We weren't about rolling on niggas (ganging up on them). We kept things one hundred with niggas. 'Put ya hands up' was the way you solved problems back then. If that ass got beaten, then take the loss and move on.

These clowns at my school would cry to the staff telling them I threatened them like this boy named O who said something after Pone's rumble with his man. I was in a tutoring session with Mr. Perry when he walked past the classroom making gestures. I came out and we rumbled. Mr. Perry came to break it up and got hit in the face. My teacher Perry told the disciplinarian what happened and I wasn't suspended.

The staredowns got worse between me and those sophomores including the females who rolled with these cats. One morning, I accidentally stepped on the back of a girl shoe and she went off. I called her a 'bitch' and she went to the disciplinarian. I got suspended for three days without even him hearing my side of the story.

———

A week later, there was a big rumble at Olney Transportation Center involving many schools. As it was going on, I was walking inside the Terminal and saw some Central High students involved. I went downstairs to the train platform going about my business. Once my train came, a girl called me out for not fighting for our school and I told her to chill. She kept shouting and it was straight-up embarrassing. My train's doors closed, and I sat down watching her rant seeing the girl was basically dickriding. I told myself if this door opens, *I will teach her little ass a lesson.* Sure enough, the train paused and a few seconds later, the doors opened again. I went up to the girl and said, "What the fuck you keep talking about?" Then, my fist landed.

I walked away confused and headed back upstairs. The boy from the fight a few days ago grabbed me from behind and we were now fighting on the steps. The train cops came rushing in and quickly arrested us. While doing so, an officer's boot was on my neck on the metal steps. There were a number of students in handcuffs; all lined up on their knees once they took us upstairs. *A brother can't catch a break for shit.*

I was taken to the 35th Police District a few blocks away and happen to be put in the cell with the pretty boys from school. "Why you hit shorty," they asked. I told them I was minding my business and she stepped to me. Surprisingly, they agreed the girl was out of pocket. A few hours later, we were released in time for supper. I was slapped with a disorderly conduct charge and later, it got dismissed.

Back in school the next day and I got suspended again even though the incident happened elsewhere. My parents were fed up and pleaded with me to stop the nonsense. *"Why now? Eric. You have a year left. Don't fuck your life up. You're at the best school in the city."* They didn't understand that I wasn't looking for trouble, it just found me. There were no one who I looked at as a role model not even my father. However, his friends would often intervene. If I were fucking up, they'd tell me. But in the back of my mind, the street life was the only way to handle this shit. I just had to outdo these cats one way or the other.

———

A few weeks before the school year ended, the principal and head disciplinarian called my parents requesting for a meeting. I had a gun from one of my homies to deal with the drama at school and took it with me that day. The drama was driving me to the point of letting off some heat if they didn't stop with the bullshit. Mom-Bev didn't know, but I felt the disciplinarian senses something when he told me to take off my coat at the meeting. I refused, and he continued asking me if I was okay. Minutes later, he asked me to step out of the room to talk with my stepmom alone.

The meeting went on and it was all about my run-ins with the other kids and my behavior throughout the year. They left me with two choices; expulsion or transfer. Number two was obvious and the only choice I had in going to school to finish out my high school tenure was Simon Gratz. Mom-Bev begged for me to finish out my final year at Central, but the principal rejected the idea. Her belief was I'd be in trouble as much as I was at Central, but it wound up being the opposite.

———

In the summer of my final year, I started working at McDonald's on Broad and Hunting Park. Everybody from the hood used to show up begging to get hooked up. The cashiers were in there hustling making deals along with the managers. At work, there were two Puerto Rican guys cooking on the grill always yelling, "Cayeti and Punyeta" every time they were joking around with the blacks on shift. I didn't realize what they were saying until later on.

At this gig, I met my homie Major AKA Major Damage. We used to get high after work. This nigga used to get so high you'd have to take him home. He started fucking with this Puerto Rican joint from the job and they moved in together down Erie Avenue. I tried coming at one of her girlfriends when I stayed over one night and the girl was straight frontin'. I had another friend at the gig named Fareed who used to come by and cut my hair. My man had skills. He also hooked me with this girl from around his way down North that had a crazy ass body but was scared to smash.

Pone and I started getting serious about this rap thing. We made demo after demo; sometimes three in a day. Pone had some homies from up North and through him, I met Kay who had the dopest Honda ever. His joint was grayish-lavender that sparkled and had pink neon lights underneath. After Kay, Pone introduced me to the Logan squad; Chris, Sa, and others that were real niggas. *This game as we understood it was to never let someone have something on you or over you.*

———

School was different at Simon Gratz. I left behind several buddies at Central that were close. My man "Soup", Dell, Roy & Pee were my homies. With my man "Soup, we'd hang out in HP (Hunting Park) and knew many of the same people from around the way. He was a rapper as well and when he dropped this joint "Co-rock a Party", I was a fan. I went to one of their rehearsals at his DJ's house, and that guy was a legend. I wish I could remember his name. Later on, I found out Soup was a cousin to my girlfriend at Central who'd already graduated and was starting her first year at Spellman.

We were still together but the long-distance thing started kicking in. When she started college, our communication started fading. She told me that she was going to a Warithud-Deen Masjid and gushed about eating halal now and living an Islamic lifestyle. I was cool with that. One day, out of the blue, she told me we couldn't talk anymore and I wanted to know why. She said she was interested in marrying the Imam (spiritual head in the community) there. I was hurt not knowing what had happened. A few months away and now she's getting married? What the hell! By the time, I told her I was interested in Islam, it was too late.

———

Back to life at Simon Gratz, I had little time to dwell on

what I couldn't control. E as they call had to find out what he was made of. I started sporting nappy hair, baggy jeans and wearing Timberlands daily. I was in the Afro-cultural thing and my fashion style reflected it. My new school buddies from the Crossroads program; Rob and James wore the same. In this program, we focused on Performing Arts. NBA basketball champion, Rasheed Wallace was also in the program. In Spanish class with Mr. Rob, he made us laugh. The school loved him, and homie always had a good heart.

Rasheed led the basketball team to the top of the nation that year. Recruits and the NBA scouts attended games and there was a lot of media coverage. I went to our championship game at the Civic Center when we won that year. As known, he's famous for the quote, "The ball don't lie."

Before coming to Gratz, I thought Craig Wise from Central was the best baller in the city, averaging 31.5 points per game until I saw Rasheed up close. Craig went to D-2 or D-3 school which was shocking and never made it to the pros.

My new school was a place of refuge from the abyss of the cold streets and our teachers were always concerned about our well-beings. I saw students cry for help and school was a home to many of us. Yeah, we had some bad apples but even they kept the bullshit on the low while in class.

I made the honor roll in my first report and my parents were proud. We all knew Gratz was easier than Central but honestly it felt like I really belong there. One of our most beloved instructors, Ms. Pincus, who taught us playwright connected our stories of experience and got us to produce dramas and plays. The urban issues such as teenage pregnancy, music, street life, and inner feelings were most of what we wrote about. It gave us a shoulder to cry on.

———

Hip-hop was jumpin' in the year of 1992. Dr. Dre released Deep Cover introducing Snoop Doggy Dogg. You'll always remember the chorus line, "187 to mutha-fuckin' cop." Mom-Bev and Dad gave me some leeway since I was doing well in school. My man Kea and I still were hooking up on the weekends and we started going to his church on Friday nights for an event called "Teen Challenge." There were some good-looking church girls in the house. Kea and I were there checking out the bitties (girls). As said, church girls are the most innocent.

Two years ago when I first got arrested, Kea's

family didn't want me around him. There was this perception that I was this troublemaker. My stepmom used to tell the neighborhood everything about me. Shit, all the kids were sneaking around doing shit but everyone knew about Eric's dirty laundry.

Yet, I had musical talent and started picking up DJ gigs around the way and beyond. I was still on thin ice with Kea's folks but they allowed me to talk to him on his porch. I couldn't come inside though. Anyway, during my days at Gratz, I was freestyling at lunch with my homies venting out my frustrations. The listeners would bang beats on the lunch tables and everyone dropped bars. I had them.

After school, you'd find me up in my room practicing and putting tracks together. All the DJ competitions inspired me, but I didn't have 1200 Technics. When Juice came out in 1991, it was even more inspiration. Whenever I had money, I'd go up to Germantown and Chelten or 11th and Filbert to buy albums. My collection was growing, and I even used some of my father's old albums in the basement. He had classic soul stuff like the Stylistics, Aretha Franklin, Teddy Pendergrass, and others from the 60s and 70s. I'd do my best with the equipment I had and my man Rob from Gratz had a beat machine, so sometimes we'd collaborate.

Rob lived around the corner from me and he had some girls on his block that kept checking me out. One girl, I started seeing but we only talked on the phone or on her couch if I could make it there. She was scared to come to my crib cos she knew what would happen.

Whenever Pone and the crew came through, we'd be like dons, blowing bud on the way to Stenton Park. You already know the deal. Pone knew cats from out the Yunk around my way. These guys were about that money and got high in style. I'd hang out with them and felt that hood loyalty. We'd talk about making money while drinking Elephant Beer and smoking jays. That beer wasn't cheap. It was like nine dollars for a six-pack of Elephant Beer back in '92-93. In the hood, the most down-low cats were the ones getting money.

During the warm months, house parties were poppin' off left and right around Nicetown, Logan, and Hunting Park sections of the city. The girls would come through from all over and we even had weekly ones at Baba's house on my block. I ran into everybody even from grade school at his parties. My boy JP came down and turned one of the dirtiest girls in Mayfair into one of the best looking. Unbelievable!

Uptown was the place to be back in '92-93. Just stay away from 5th and Fairhill. You'd see smokers and dealers on the block like it was a flea market. Cops would ride up but there was nothing they could do or ordered to do. Here and there, there were busts but tricking and addicts were still working overtime from Old York Road & Erie Avenue on down to HP.

I started messing with Black mixed with Puerto Rican joint with a crazy body from HP. When she came one day, my neighbor came right behind and rang my doorbell. He knew the shit and found out he was talking to her as well. I hate to say it but *bitches ain't shit.*

My final high school days were winding down and I started going out with another girl with these sexy brown eyes from down North. I would see her in the hall and she would ask why I wasn't fucking with her although I was. She'd grabbed me and kiss me and that would end her interrogation. Sadly, we never hooked up outside of school.

On Tuesdays, Gratz had a peer group and I had

joined. We talked about our everyday problems and sought solutions. Our instructor was so gorgeous. I wonder if I can call her a MILF? Anyway, I was still up in the air about what university to go to but studying out-of-state was my first priority. There was nothing in Philly I hadn't seen before.

Clark University Atlanta was my first option followed by Hampton University. In the late 1980s and early 1990s, Blacks were heading back down South. The lower cost of living and job opportunities particularly the upcoming Olympics in Atlanta were the main attractive points. The out-of-state tuition around that time ($7,600 per semester) was an issue for my folks and they weren't trying to cough up the dough. I had about five thousand dollars in grant monies which would get me more than half of the way. Still, my folks wouldn't budge. I was then compelled to pick a local school to my list and chose Lincoln University. I applied for a few scholarships at the Free Library on Vine Street and with my school counselor throughout the year hoping that I still could make the Atlanta move.

Weirdly enough, I was also reading about several religions on my lunch breaks. Animalism caught my eye because it associated your actions back to your ancestors. I tried lighting up a few candles in my bedroom to pray to them a few times and nothing happened. I lost faith in it instantly.

When everyone was getting ready for the prom, I wasn't. It honestly never came to my mind until I started writing my story. Life was about hip-hop, basketball, girls, working and getting high. My man, Fu who lived two houses down from Kea was the perfect example of what the hood should represent. He was a clean-cut brother who had this fondness for wearing silver. The girls were on him and he rolled solo and enjoyed being fly. A few doors down, we'd be on Kea's porch hanging out cracking on the girls that walked by. Then, the house parties started happening at this Jamaican boy's house on the weekends. The girls came through, but the parties weren't hitting like that. A new neighbor moved next to Kea who resembled a version of Adina Howard but slimmer. We'd talk and hit it off for a bit. When her brother came home from jail, my crew and his had a little run-in after some words. Kea's father came outside in his underwear carrying a shotgun, telling everyone to chill out. The man used to be a football player and he was no joke.

———

Finally, it was graduation day and all of my classmates

were looking super fresh. The ceremony was held down at Temple University and my relatives on both sides showed up and took many photos. This was the beginning of being that master as great-grandma always mentioned in her letters to me. I was shaken that day as the crowd filled the air with cheers and whistles. When Rasheed Wallace's name was called, everyone went insane.

Now, it feels so good to be a high school graduate. The class of 1993 was in effect. Yet, with a few months left before college, I still have time to fool around. It's a G thang baby!

THAT HOUSE DUDE

I have to turn back the clock to around the end of my 11th-grade year despite the hardships I went through for this chapter. With the Rodney King beating and some other Black awareness stuff going on in the country, I was doing some real soul-searching.

Remember I was in Mount Airy with my play aunt and uncle because of the beef I had going on with my dad. The Olney neighborhood wasn't far from Mount Airy, so I'd go hang out at JP's house, after school to hear some new rap stuff. When Special Ed first came out, JP was like, "E this dude's the shit." Then when Lord Finesse and Poor Righteous Teachers dropped their debuts, he put me down. One evening while talking on the phone, JP asked me to go down Center City to Club Baseline with him. It would be my first time clubbing, so why not? I didn't ask my auntie for money because I didn't want her to know what where I was going. Once me and JP got to the door, the stupidest thing happened. I didn't have enough dough to get inside, so we left. What a setback!

The following weekend I came correct. I'm not sure if I went with JP or my play cousin but all I know it was marvelous. The DJ played Rap, Reggae, and House throughout the evening and I even tried dancing. Everybody was having a good time and getting it in. The bass that came through the speakers made your ears shake. The ladies were deep and I started dancing with this jawn from West Philly forgetting all about who was with me. That booty kept sliding up and down on me. I left around three in the morning and once I got home, I fell asleep in my clothes.

Later in the day, I called the girl seeing if she wanted to see me. She suggested we hook up on the following weekend. At her grandmother's house, she kept playing those little games with my thing while her grandma was facing away from us. When grandma left the room, it was on but the girl didn't want the whole package.

The following weekend, she came up to Mount

Airy and called me a freak because I trying to get some. Don't know why because she was leading me on. Anyway, once she left, I may have seen her once again but it was at her school. Things weren't going nowhere, so we stop talking. The girl was cute though.

For the next two weekends in the row, I went down the Baseline on the solo tip, but it was popping. So, I went around town to see what's going on with the other clubs. My boy Kea was down. I found the Trocadero had it going on Friday and Saturday nights. Kea was frontin' at first about going down there because he wanted only Rap and Reggae. I didn't care as long as the bitties were in the house.

Before we went to the Trocadero, Kea discovered a nightclub called the Night on Broadway up around JP's neighborhood. All Kea talked about was how many phone numbers we'd set out to get. That was our little competition thing back in the day. Once we got settled up in the club, Kea had this jawn (girl) sitting on his lap while my number count was still at zero. By the time the night was over which was around midnight, we'd tally up the count and Kea came out with more. *My man!*

Kea still wasn't convinced about going to the Trocadero though. He missed the Bassline before it closed down but one Friday, he decided to give the Troc a go. The club was so crowded that the line swung around the corner and some. We had some drinks before we got in and once we did, it felt like we were inside an auditorium. The place was humongous. The house music was bumpin' and Kea hated it. I was dancing with this Italian girl and we were kissing and grinding for more than an hour; taking breaks and shit. The girl was tight, dawg. I got her number and hit her up the following day and her sister cock-blocked acting like she didn't speak English. *What the fuck!*

Earlier in the morning, my parents asked what time I came in. I was back on Carlisle Street after me and my dad's fight. My response was "Midnight," and sure enough they knew I was lying.

The summer of 1993 was the year the Greek Picnic was at Belmont Plateau and it was the shit. Everyone was dancing in the grass and having a good time. Bud was lit and everyone sang along with DJ. Philly Police was around, scoping but letting all of us enjoy ourselves. If you were over sixteen, you came out for the Greek. Girls wore coochie-cutters (shorts that showed a lot of ass) and they'd be riding on the back of motorcycles. The guys came geared up and all the city's ballers were on the scene. If you walked through enough of the park, you'd see people having sex inside of cars, bushes or wherever. Many times they were being videotaped.

Weeks before the Greek, Philly annually hosts the Odunde festival on the 2nd Saturday in June. My mom would have a stand down there and I'd come by and chill out with her. People from all over came and South Street would be crowded. They'd play House Music, Rap and Reggae throughout the day and people would shop or just have mad fun. I listened to enough rap and reggae but house music is what had me going. I remember trying to learn how to dance to it in Mount Airy when no one was home. Unfortunately, I didn't have no rhythm. When I was tired, I'd throw on some Anita Baker, Lisa Lisa or one of my rap albums.

DOIN' IT UP ON CAMPUS

CHAPTER EIGHT

I was ready to hit campus willing to take the next step to adulthood on my terms. Yet, there is a difference between being mature and not.

In the middle of August 1993, freshmen like myself were arriving at colleges for orientation. At the check-in, we headed straight to the financial aid office and saw that I owed $868. I was told it's on you. After pleading with financial aid, they told me I can stay on campus for thirty days until I pay it off. I turned to my folks and they told me straight out "It's on you, son. We can't afford to take out any loans." Those words hurt me and it took years before I let it go. *"Pay the damn bill and let me live,"* were my thoughts.

While settling in the McRary Dorms, I wondered what if I couldn't pay off my tuition. *What would I do next? Couldn't go back home because my parents didn't want me there. Maybe I'll stay on campus and see how things play out.*

My dorm was co-ed and when I arrived, I had the room to myself. A few days later, a guy from DC showed up messing up my groove. After we finished orientation mid-day, I'd head to the back of the dorms to smoke some weed. A couple days later, I met a bro named Miz from Philly who was already puffing in the same spot. Miz introduced me to Riz, Dee, and Tee; all freshmen like myself from Philly. We didn't have classes together, but when we got out; we sure got high. Still, the tuition issue was still lingering in the back of my mind.

When Miz and I talked about hip hop, I found it strange he believed Brand Nubian was the best rap group out. I couldn't agree when you had MC Ren, Dr. Dre, Ice Cube, Gravediggers, Wu-Tang Clan, Public Enemy, Das Efx, Krs-One, Eric B & Rakim, Kool G Rap and the Hit Squad killin' it. Shit, you had some gangsta rappers that was killing it too; NWA, Snoop Doggy Dogg, Lady of Rage, Dogg Pound, Scarface, Geto Boys, MC Breed, MC Eiht, DJ Quick, Compton's Most Wanted and others. Nevertheless, I gave everybody a fair play such as Apache, Sweet Tee, MC Hammer, Professor Griff, and other one-hit wonders. My baby sister often teases me about listening to Twin Hype.

———

A week passed by and I felt so free. Two girls from Philly hooked up with us and we were scheming on getting in dark skin jawn's panties. Miz smashed and how I found out is when Dee told me. That nigga is slick.

When I wasn't with the crew, I'd in my room practicing my DJ skills. My roommate from DC would go mad, saying "Can you turn it down, please? I need to study." My response was, "We're out of school now, so chill out." A few days later after us arguing back and forth, he switched dorm rooms. Best of regards.

The days were counting down on paying off my tuition balance. A notice from the school left under my dorm room door said if I didn't have pay in 14 days, I'd have to vacate. With each day counting down, I continued partying harder, saying, "Fuck it. It is what it is."

In my third week on campus, Lincoln University hosted a hip-hop competition inside the school's cafeteria. The neighboring institutions; Cheyney, Millersville, and West Chester were part of the competition causing over a hundred students to be in the house. I tried teaming up with Miz, but he got cold feet. I went solo and freestyled to Deep Cover's instrumental. There was a mix of boos and haa's but I didn't rehearse beforehand.

The deadline was approaching fast and I just said, "Fuck it. Where are the ladies?" There were two I was peeping; one from Maryland and the other from Pittsburgh. Pittsburgh was gorgeous but wasn't budging. Maryland, on the other hand, wanted to cuddle up but didn't want to smash. I don't blame her either. *Shit, get that education while you're single.*

The day came when I had to leave campus. I gave my guys hugs and told them I'd be back. When I got back to Philly, I started looking for work right away. UPS was hiring and I applied. A week later, I got hired. After work, I'd go by a neighbor's house across the street who was a few years older than me. We'd drink, smoke a little weed and watch sports. Another neighbor would come after work but he didn't drink or smoke. My man always had jokes though.

On the weekends, we'd hit up the neighborhood bars and nightclubs like the Princess Lounge and Sid

Bookers. Nothing heavy but we mostly had a good time.

I started seeing this thick tall jawn from Hunting Park who was sixteen, emancipated and had her own crib. She used to come by and my parents were cool with it as long as we weren't fuckin' in the house. Word! One weekend, I was ill and when she had stopped past, I tried being slick. We had plans to go out that evening, but I told her I was staying in. Stupidly, I asked her for some money and her bus pass and she hooked me up. As soon as she left, I got dressed and left. The girl was pissed off at me for saying one thing and doing another. From there, things went south.

———

Getting high began to affect my decision-making. Around the last week of September of the year of 1993, I paid for it dearly. Some homies and I were cruising around and they were looking for trouble. I was in the backseat alone high as shit when they stuck up some white dudes at Drexel University. When they heard the cops, they left the car in the middle of the street and started running. I got out a minute later trying to assess what the hell was going on. Police sirens were buzzing from every direction. I panicked and ran, high as a kite until I was out of breath. The cops surrounded me and drew their weapons. Next thing I know I was in handcuffs.

I got charged with robbery and aggravated assault just weeks away from my eighteenth birthday. Wrong place and perhaps perfect timing. The cops held me at the police station on 55th and Vine for three days as I rotted away on cheese sandwiches and ice tea. I lied about my age, hoping to get out on ROR (released on recognition). The station's chief came by the day I was hoping to get released and said I was being sent to the Detention Center even though he knew my real age. What a fucker!

I was locked away in the cell for twenty-three hours a day. The reason being that they couldn't let me out in general population due to my age. There was another youngster on the block as well who got locked up for kidnapping his baby son. His story was crazy. For that one hour we had, it was a blessing. Of course, they'd let us out for showers, checkups and phone calls. The toilets inside the cells were so cold to sit on that I held in my crap in for nearly a week. If you had cigarettes, they were worth more than money. A Muslim brother used to give me some rolled-up ones whenever I asked.

My parents never came up to DC during those

seven days of hell. My dad snapped when he found out who was with me that night that I got booked. I wasn't going to snitch. It's the code of the streets.

———

Days before I turned eighteen, I got released from jail. Pone and I got together and celebrated by getting high, drunk and dropping tracks earlier in the day. On Friday night of my birthday, there was a house party going on down the Yunk. You could feel the bass of Jazzy Jeff and Fresh Prince's song "House Party" a mile away. "E, it's your birthday man, so do you, my nigga," Pone told me as we walked through. We guzzled some Mad Dog 20/20 and blew on some chronic. Niggas were lit as fuck. Once we got to a party a few blocks away, I started dancing with the bitties. One guy was jealous and caught me in the back of the head. His crew then jumped me and I was drunk as fuck. I didn't feel shit.

Pone was fighting while I was on the ground, taking in the situation. These sucka ass niggas dared doing something like this. "We're gonna' get these motherfuckers, E." Don't even worry about it," shouted Pone as he got me up off the ground. I wasn't even hurt just fucked up from drinking.

———

I slept down Pone's spot for the rest of the weekend and headed back up North on Sunday afternoon. We were good and had a plan for those niggas. I am my brother's keeper.

Pone told me to chill from down the Yunk for a while, so we can wait for the heat to die down and other shit. I started working at UPS and the gig was strenuous. We loaded hundreds of packages per shift and UPS recorded how fast we sorted. Thankfully, the morning shift went by quickly and all that mattered was getting back to Lincoln University for the next semester.

At the gig, I met a brother from Southwest Philly who said he could help me get my hustle on when I got back to school. You know I was down for whatever. I got some killer weed from one of his connects and that's all she wrote.

THE REBOUND

CHAPTER NINE

My parents were trippin' and I was becoming harder to control. Between hustling, working part-time, and a partial scholarship from the Concerned Role Models organization, I was good to go for my homecoming semester at Lincoln.

When I got back to school, the weather was hawking. I was switched to McQuary Dorm with the boys this time around. Most of the squad from Philly was still on campus but there were new newbies and a few shorties. The jawn Miz smashed, didn't come back for the spring semester!

People called me "Cee" on campus. When Pone nicknamed me "Cotton", I just ran with it. The reason why I was "C" because I used to smoke cigarettes down to the filter.

"What's up, Cee? We know you brought some of that Philly chronic back?" the homies asked.

"No doubt, my nigga for sure."

My new roommate was from Brooklyn and he was cool as shit. A straight dread boy from Brooklyn. That nigga wouldn't stop freestyling even when the track was over when he was high as crap. Since I had the bud from Southwest, the clientele came through all times of the day and night. If I was out, Pee manned the ship. There were a few dudes hustling out there but we had the best weed. I had a little dispute with one of the dealers from Philly but it was all love. I copped from him for my personal stash even though his shit was ass most of the time. I just wasn't into smoking mine.

Females from DC, Maryland, Virginia, Carolina, and other cities would come up to our dorm room to hang out. The Alpha Phi Alpha Fraternity room was right down the hall and our squad was deeper than we had in the fall semester. Twenty deep at least and others from New York, DC, Pittsburgh, Connecticut, and even LA were all in the gang. It was a gangsta party.

The girls on campus came from all over the states; DC, Maryland, Virginia, Carolinas, Chicago, Cali and even the Bahamas. We had bitties up in our room daily getting high as shit and buying. With the Alpha Phi

Alpha room down the hall, it was lovely. The Philly squad got deeper and we had things in check on campus. Dudes from New York, DC, Pittsburgh, Connecticut, and even LA gave us love and it was surely a gangsta party.

The best time of my life had to be living on campus. My roommate, Pee and I had those red-light parties going on in our door rom. The chronic was blazin' and the business was booming. "Gin and Juice" was the anthem on campus. My man Gee from Connecticut came with some gin and fruit punch. We drank a few cups of it and told him it was weak. He came back with a mix that put our asses down. That same night, the Alphas down the hall was throwing a party and the girls were comin' through. I was done watching the weed haze filling the hallways. I kept the red light in the room for the ladies to come through. This joint from the Southside came by I vomited right before she slid through. I was too fucked up to even comprehend what was going on.

———

It was hawking outside and the heating system in our dorm had broken down. It was so cold we covered our radiators and windows to keep whatever heat we could in. On top of that, the halls and bathrooms were dirty as shit from what took place on the weekends. The maintenance people were off on the weekends and most of the time, you had to go to the women's dorms to take a shower.

Right before the major snowstorm of 1994, my homies Miz, Riz, and I were walking through the back of the boys' dorms, looking for a spot to smoke. Riz was already high as shit insisting on rolling up a blunt in the dark. Miz and I told him to chill but that nigga wouldn't listen. When we stopped to wait for him to finish rolling, the dude dropped the blunt in the grass. Some campus security came right up and told us to follow them. We begged them but they weren't trying to hear anything.

We sat in Dr. Boroughs' office (the head disciplinarian) for what seemed like ages. Dr. Boroughs was from North Philly and was tough. He knew Riz's folks which probably helped us a lot. He told us to write a letter home informing our parents about what we did. If they didn't sign it, we'd be suspended. He also said the next time we had drugs on campus, we'd be expelled. My parents were pissed but that didn't stop me from smoking. Riz was scared to death.

As the semester was halfway through, I had trouble with one of my classes over something silly. My homie Tee and I stayed in because a blizzard hit our area the morning of our midterms. My first class was canceled, so I assumed my second would be too. That class was African Studies and our instructor was a Nigerian man whose words were hard to get. I found out on the next class that he came and requested for a makeup. The teacher refused and since he gave only a midterm and final, there was no need for me to continue attending his class. In my other classes, I had no difficulties.

If the weather lightened up, my crew and others played basketball near the girls' dorms. One night was so hilarious. We were falling all over the place, high as shit.

———

After classes ended, sometimes we'd go to the Quad to watch the fraternities and sororities perform their steps. The AKA girls were all redbones and man, they looked good as fuck.

The girls in our Philly squad were crazy. After class, they'd sneak off to the bleachers to puff some herb and be acting like they didn't have any weed but wanted to smoke ours up. One was a straight weed head and the other would be done after a few puffs. She'd be giggling so hard it seemed like she was choking to death. Both of them were from the Logan section of Philly.

A week later, one boy from Connecticut who smoked bud for the first time was so high that he jumped out the 2nd-floor window. Luckily, he survived. That dude didn't come back to school after that. Shit, that must have been some good ass weed.

———

A dude name G from Sharon Hill hooked me up with jams that weren't even out on the market yet. I even heard Kurupt from the Dogg Pound old joints when he was rhyming with his homies back East over his spot. Back at the pad, my roommate was pumping MC Breed's new joint, "The New Breed." That joint was slamming. K- Solo dropped his 2nd album; "King of the Mountain" while Wu-Tang Clan's debut: "Enter the 36 Chambers" dropped. My homies from Connecticut put me down with Black Moon's debut joint, "Enter the Stage" which was fire. Sadly, after a month, my roommate left Lincoln and went back to New York. We did it up big for him before he bounced. *One love always my nigga.*

———

"Out of order" signs were hung up on Monday mornings in the bathrooms after the weekend-partying. Toilet paper and trash was all over the hallways. The dorm's heating system was back on but was off and on. A lot of my homies complained and was thinking about going back home at the end of the semester. We were tired of living in a small ass town with nothing to do on campus.

A few weeks later, my boy Vee from North got busted for having beedies (cigarettes wrapped in leaves). Campus security searched the dorms looking for drugs and alcohol early Monday morning. Although Vee's cigarettes had no weed in them, Dr. Boroughs still warned him about having them and confiscated them. Some others on campus got caught selling forties, weed and other stuff and they got kicked out. Happily, I was out of weed when the raids went down.

Tee who was from our squad was fed up, too. He used to look out for the brothers when our cash was low. He didn't smoke weed but he drank his ass off. Being broke on campus was a bitch. Some of us went a whole month without having money. Our friend, Dee started a loan-shark business and I was tempted to borrow but never did.

————

Everyone got along with the guy called Cee which is (me). I was down for whatever. Not everyone was fortunate to go home on the weekends including me. If I could, I'd hitch a ride. My parents weren't making that trip up to Lincoln. One weekend, I went back to Philly with a guy who went to Central with me but graduated two years before my class. On the way back to Lincoln, we got into a car accident on 69th Street in Upper Darby. I was shaken up and we got out of the car, the other driver's car was busted up pretty badly. Fortunately, my man's car didn't have a scratch.

Another time, Miz's father brought me back to Philly. Miz, Dee and I got high before leaving and were quiet during the trip back. Once we got back, we went to Miz's house first and were invited inside. Once inside, there was this calming presence that I've never experienced before. Dee and I felt it and were amazed. We sobered up quickly and took it all in.

————

Now, that the winter semester was coming to an end, most of my friends went on to study at our local college, CCP. We were fed up with Lincoln even if they promised to upgrade the campus. Still, it wasn't enough for me to consider going back although I did for Lincoln's homecoming the next semester. Some stuff improved, but it still was the same ole. Dee and I took a ride up there with an ounce of skunk (weed). We smoked it with our boys who stayed behind. On the way up I-95, the car was smoking from so much weed exhaled out the windows. Inside, we were bumping Smif-N-Wessun, Wu-Tang, and the Gravediggers.

THE HUSTLE DON'T STOP

CHAPTER TEN

Being back in Philly now, it was not what I expected. Dad didn't want me at home and my baby sister took over my room. My mom, however, was open to letting me stay with her. I visited her a few times on the weekends while I was at Lincoln and we began bonding.

The first few months went smooth. I ate, woke up when I wanted and stayed without paying rent. It was like night and day coming from the Northwest section of the city to living down in the heart of it. Prostitution, drugs, ran-down homes and trash was the landscape of most of the neighborhoods in my new area. I began messing with this girl from 24th Street. We hit it off a few times and the girl got me for some dough fast forward a few years later. I was asleep after doing what we do and she went into my closet and got me.

The girl left before I woke up. Maybe she might have been smokin'. *Don't let me catch yo black ass. LOL.*

Anyway, one of my friends from Lincoln lived a few blocks away from my mother. When we visited Philly, he had introduced me to a few of his associates who were hustlers. These dudes were getting money on the low.

Mom started bitching about me going back to school and demanded I enroll for the upcoming semester. I tried but missed the deadline. In the meantime, I would be up in the house playing video games, blasting rap music and smoking weed not doing shit. I brought my DJ equipment from Lincoln to my mom's crib and was going rogue in my bedroom.

When I went by my mom's mom apartment, she gave me money and advice. She always said, "A man should always have a dollar in his pocket." My grandmother loved basketball and her favorite team was the Los Angeles Lakers. "Kobe Bryant will be great one day," she said all the time and it turns out her prediction was correct. With the money Nana gave me, I'd waste it on weed and get-high. At this point in my life, I was far from being responsible.

My father's side was opposite to mother's. They were caring, but asking for money was off-limits. Dad often reminded me to call my grandmother and go by to see her even when we were at war. Both of my grandfathers passed away before my teenage years and my memories of them are not many.

———

Most of my childhood friends were still on Carlisle Street and living in Nicetown. I tried going inside my dad's house to get some stuff but I wouldn't be let in except for a few times by my baby sister. Unfortunately, I was threatened to get it out of there or it would get thrown in the trash. Regardless, I stuck to my goal of staying in school and not trying to work at a fast-food joint. Selling drugs was an option but I was trying to stay clean. Nevertheless, there was a way around that by going down to the 3-2 Center for public assistance which is now known as the welfare office.

I was looking rough, I admit that day. Hair was unkempt and my goatee was wild looking. For years, I kept my old 1994 welfare ID card to remind how far I had come. When I went in and explained my situation, I was told what to say to the caseworker before going and didn't lie about my situation. There was a checkbox stating whether or now you were using drugs? If you marked yes, they would give you food stamps and cash and if not, they'd likely deny you.

Minutes later, I was told to pick my welfare check at a check-cashing spot off of 2nd and Frankford Ave on the 4th day of the month.

Walking down Lehigh Avenue back to Mom's house, I started feeling this tingle. A chick I met down 22nd and Lehigh from West Philly burnt me. That ass was nice but shorty got me even with a rubber on. The next day, I went down Broad and Lombard and got that shot. Nothing major but that shit hurt. The clinic gave out a free bag of Lifestyles. *All you had to do was ask.*

Meanwhile, I caught up with my boy from Lincoln to look into hustling. *Things need to happen now.* He put some logistics in place and we'd split half of the profits. His area was a dead zone. Smokers were out there but no one was really buying. We reminisced on our days back at Lincoln while smoking bud before we started our shift. The money is what we needed to keep our school dreams alive. I didn't want to be a full-time hustler. I only wanted to get what was mine.

———

Our partnership was tight even though I wasn't the one in charge of the money. My man set up the places where we could make money without being out on the corners. Sometimes, we did twelve-hour shifts and only made seventy-five dollars. A few dealers were nickel-and-diming out there but it was like a desert. Our frustration grew, but we reminded each other to remain patient.

I hustled in spots where smokers, city workers, retirees, and prostitutes would hang out. You'd be surprised on who would come through. Some women came through that you couldn't even tell they were smoking blow.

There was a lookout at one of the dope houses named Gee. He was a dependable oldhead. He brought you clientele he considered as big spenders and sometimes some badass chicks. There were times, smokers would come with VCRs, TVs, stereos and other shit looking to get a fix. We had it all.

———

Out of the blue after two months or so, my partner decided we should link up with this dude who was dealing meth. That guy wasn't serious about making money and loved showing off. Hooking-up with this cat wasn't worth it. A deal got cut with this boa (guy in Philly dialect) regardless and he started mixing his meth in our dope. Smokers began complaining the shit was too strong. Within a week, we had to shut our operation down. We lost most of our dope and found out we didn't make much money either. I think I stepped off with about $600.

Before our downfall, Dee and I got a membership at Bally's on 15th and Market. Healthy minds bring healthy results, right? We talked about accepting Islam once we gave up hustling. Sometimes, I'd bring the Holy Quran with me and sit in the jacuzzi; reading it while talking to the lifeguard. I was at peace even the women were around in bikinis with their ass cheeks hanging out. While there, I met an older Muslim brother who usually came in when I was leaving. He sold oils and used to drop science on me in the locker room. His talks almost made me think about what would happen after death.

———

Whenever I had a chance to get away from Northside, I'd be down South Philly. 4th Street was bumping and I'd come through. My cuz Pone linked with the people down there and I started grinding. Puerto Ricans, Whites, Blacks, Italians, Koreans, and Cambodians all lived in that hood and everyone had a hustle; syrup, pills, weed, coke or whatever. We had niggas on that strip just in case anything went down. Still, you had to keep your eyes open for anything. There were stick-up boys out there trying to eat like you and if they caught you slippin', it was a rap. One of them got me one morning when I was just hitting the strip. I was packin' so it was just give up the goods. This nigga particularly carried around two nines, looking for money. Sometimes, he'd ride pass standing on the back of a pickup truck just to let you know I'm around. My cuz was like, "you'll learn."

This hustling stuff was short-lived and I was considering accepting Islam once it was all over. No one I rolled with was into buying fancy cars, clothes, or jewelry. Just had to be nice to the neighbors to keep things going smoothly. All they wanted was a drama-free block and respect. Most of them would look out for you on the strength of keeping order.

I never posted up on the corner for long. *Keep your back to the wall and eyes open.* I was moving a pack or sometimes two a day, but I was wanted more. My cut was quarter off of each and the shit was good. One of the most drug syndicates of our city founded that spot and I was walking in the shadows of their relatives who took over.

When I had time off which was mainly on the weekends, I took the Patco train down Camden to make a little cash on the side. My old girl from high school was from there and it was the spot to buy liquor for cheap. I'd buy miniature bottles of Cisco and Vodka on Haddon Avenue right off of Wildwood and take them back to Philly.

After spending a few weekends in a row down there, it was time to make some serious money. I bagged most of my weed and went down. Off of Haddon Avenue, I came across some guys sitting on steps. "I got weed." Niggas said they didn't have any money. Around seven o'clock, I started heading back to the train station when the same guys started following me. One boy no older than thirteen rode past me on a bike and I started walking faster until I reached a beauty salon. I dipped inside thinking these cats wouldn't go inside and sure enough, they did. Women screamed and they came rushing after me. I threw the weed out to distract them and swung at one of them. Two dudes pinned me against the wall and went through my pockets, getting some cash and a few bags of weed. I got up out of there somehow and ran to the train station as fast as I could. Fortunately, they didn't follow me.

"Next stop, Lehigh Avenue and Glenwood Station," the train announcer said. I held the back of my head which was bleeding and got on the 54 bus to 29th and Lehigh. When I got to the corner where I was hustling, the boss was out there grinding with his partner. "What happened to you, Cee?" he asked.

"I was in Camden hustling and those niggas got me."

"Cee, are you crazy? I live down there and I don't even hustle there. Good thing you got out alive. Them niggas are killers."

"Al hamdulilah."

So far, I escaped death twice in the drug game. There may be no third time.

———

The fall was approaching fast and money was on my mind. I put in extra work and kept my gear fresh. My mom was cool just doing her own thing. I was eatin' (getting money) and nobody knew a thing. I was now on night shift but keeping my eyes open with the 357 Magnum. I wasn't trying to be a gunslinger but it is what it is.

Most of the customers were cool, but you never know who was plotting. The game is deep and you have to know who the players are. You can get rocked (killed) at any moment and you'll be another statistic. Everybody out there has self-interest including yourself.

On one of my shifts, I was watching the dope house and catching traffic outside with one smoker as the lookout. When I stepped out, she came in. For a few minutes, I was smoking a Newport and while doing so, a guy in a hoodie ran up and poked me with what I believed was a gun. "I don't have anything, yo," I countered. My gun was about a foot away in a flower pot. All I had to do was stand up and it was on. "Get up and empty your pockets." I stood slowly, grabbed the 357 and aimed at his head.

"If you kill this nigga, you're going to hell and jail."

The guy was begging for his life. "Please don't kill me." I was about to press the trigger but I got spiritual. "Go, yo, go."

That nigga ran off with the quickness into the night.

———

I was still shaken up the next morning when I woke up. *Shit, I was about to kill a man.* Before I started my next shift, I talked about it with some of my associates on the corner then I went back home to shower. I came down a bit early and met up with my man from Lincoln and one of the bosses. They were sitting in the car chilling, smoking a jay. The lyrics to EMPD's "Strictly Business" was playing in the background. I took a drag and the weed was killer. So much killer, that I kept repeating the verse, "They mad at me cos they know I got cash. I'm the E-double..."

We all know that intoxicants bring out the inner truth.

The next day, I was dropped from the crew. I tried explaining but I rubbed the boss the wrong way. Actually, we're closer nowadays than ever.

Walking back to my mom's, I reflected on whether if it was time to hang this shit up for good. For the next few weeks, I thought more and more about the direction of where my life was going. I hope you take the time to read the next book of There and Now.

THERE AND NOW

VOLUME THREE

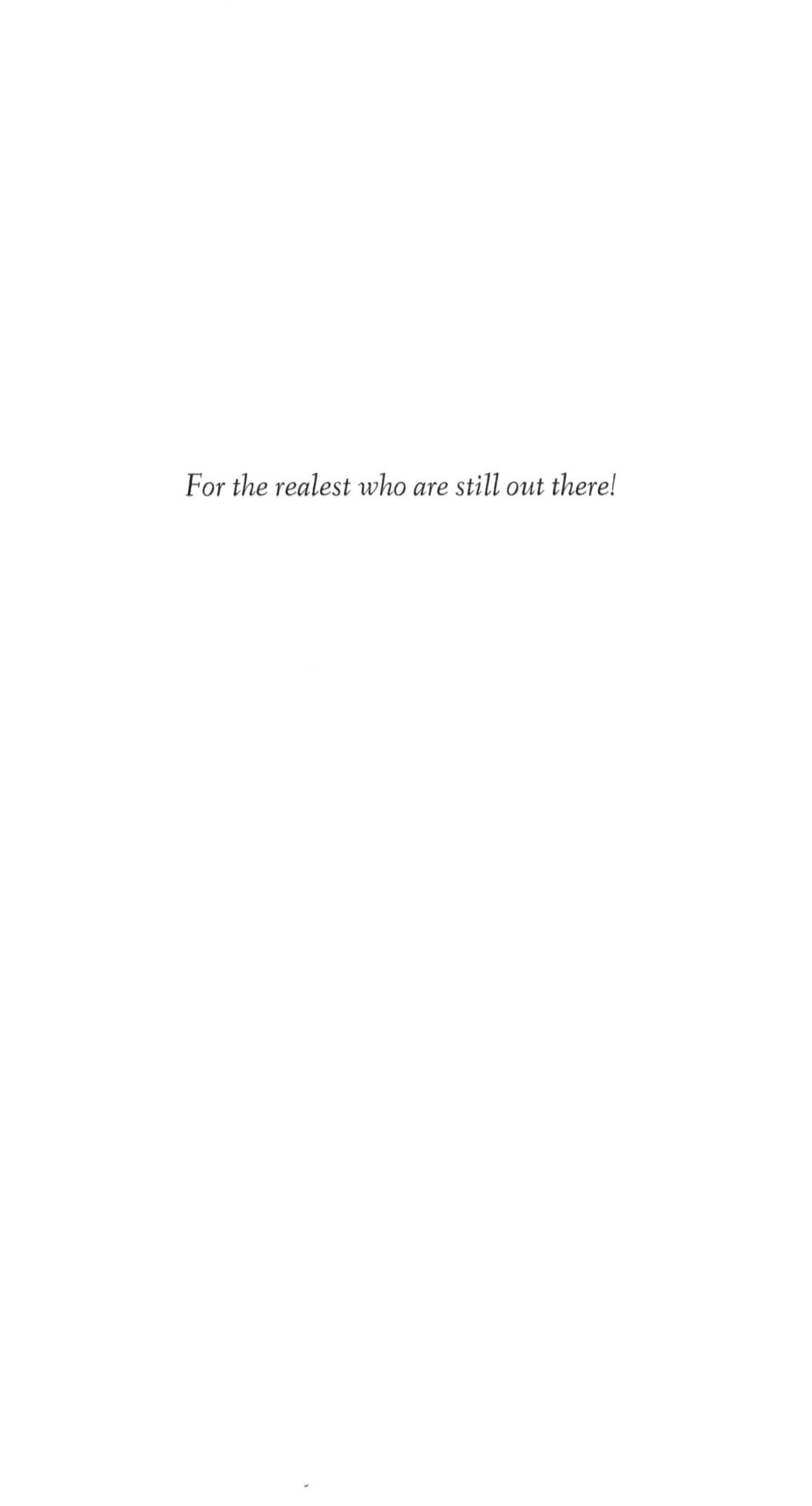

For the realest who are still out there!

I pledge allegiance to the fair and balanced truth,

> Not the bias truth,
> Not the liest truth,
> But the highest truth

— Nas

WHAT YA GONNA DO, E

Friday had to be the day. The day that I believed it would be in my best interest to take my Shahada (acceptance of Islam). I had nothing else to do after moving on from the corner. I talked it over with my older half-sibling and uncle Na. They gave me books and showed me some details on what to expect. Two of the books that I was given were from Dr. Malakai York entitled "The Book of Revelation and The Prayer of the Prophet". I found the information interesting and deep. I'd sit in the room in my mom's house for hours looking over its content, but the streets were still calling me. The game doesn't stop nor does the hustle.

Unfortunately, there was a delay in my plans, so I skipped going to the mosque for some reason. Juggling between college, mom, fallout on dad's side of the family, the dope game, women, North Philly, and getting money, my life was filled with doubts. My mom was pleased with me though and supported me with whatever she had. Days off from the dope game started to reduce my stash, however, the time off brought some needed relief and cleared my senses a bit.

Mom's neighborhood was pushing me to do what wasn't in my best interest. The addicts in the hood knew I was a hustler that didn't step on toes. There's money in the game for everyone, but greed is why n***** get slumped. I couldn't support the habits of anyone close to me. That was a challenge at times. The knocks on my door would get ignored. I would shun them or tell them I sold out. I was trying to change. I never kept anything in the house. If I left some weed in the crib, the mice used to eat the seeds and spit my buds across the floor. I'd be pissed off.

I brought my DJ equipment with me from high school and college days. I'd pump up the volume and rock the block from my window when my mom went on errands. The neighbors were cool and I kept good relationships with them. My mom's house is like an expo for all Afrocentric, organic and Muslim products. She sells items that she either made herself or bought. Oils, incense, soaps, shirts, buttons, kufis (Islamic men headgear) and much more were all on display outside at her table.

Mom would tell my bro Su and me to watch the stand when she went out on errands. My brother, Su used to hate watching the stand because he wanted to play ball with his boys up the street on the court. "Did you make any money", she'd say when she got back. We'd be like "Yeah but nothing big." She knew we were slimming. For me, I needed a nickel bag of weed and a blunt and if I were short, working at mom's stand would make up the difference. Su just needed some change to buy some junk at the store. Mom is a strong individual and knew how to survive. She knew the game. Everyone in the neighborhood still gives Mom the respect earned. She's a realist and straightforward. She doesn't hold back how she sees things. Sometimes, it got me in trouble to debate with her.

I began falling-out of favor with mom because of me hanging around the house so much and not having anything to the table on the regular. I gave up hustling for the moment and tried to focus on school. Things were getting tight around the house. I had women come over and mom knew the deal. I hit it off with one girl named Cookie who I met on the Lehigh Avenue on my way up to the crib one day. She was sitting on the porch with her girlfriend checking me out as I walked passed. I got the digits and came back later that day and it was curtains. Anyway, she was cool and used to come by mom's house to bust it up. A few years later though, I found out what how slick this joint really was by stealing some money out of my crib while I was asleep. Another story.

Met this jawn named Joy from Westside with brown eyes and tight body. We met in front of the liquor store at 22nd and Lehigh smoking some bud waiting for the 54 Bus. She was raw no doubt. Not often in my time, you see a girl by herself smoking bud. I had to crack on her. Once I did, we smoked and talked a bit. She had some peoples down 5th and Susquehanna that she often visited. I came to that spot once and thought it was a setup so I bounced early. A few nights later, she called and we met up in the park off of Germantown and Susquehanna. We played around a bit in the dark till some policeman saw us. I was startled. Cops that don't have anything to do can cause problems. She was like just chill. We stepped off and headed to the subway.

Some joints are straight freaks. The first time that a bro got burnt wasn't nice at all. I was done with her, but it wasn't easy because she said that she wasn't with messing around with anybody. I believed her at first, but when it happened the second time, I had to step off. She came by mom's crib one night and unfortunately, it was not a memorable experience.

Mom's had grown tired of me and decided it was time for me to go. I began searching for a new place while often staying with Dew at nights until I found one. I still visited my boys on the corner even though I wasn't out there anymore. My search for a room ended with one off 21st and Toronto. The room was located on the first floor next to the front door. During the daytime, the house was quiet as a mouse and at night, the roaches, the roaches, the roaches. It got worse as the days grew hotter. If I had to run out, I'd put my bed in the center of the room and plug the water hole of the iron, so they couldn't get inside. I couldn't cook in the kitchen and had to sleep in the middle of the room. After three weeks, I couldn't take it anymore. I packed and left.

Dad's house was off limits because of our strained relationship. My sisters were told not to let me in. I did convince my sisters to let me in to get some of my possessions that I left behind. My belongings were stored in the basement. The family issues with my father could have been dealt with the help of family members or professionals, but no one stepped up to address the situation.

I'm now officially homeless. Living from friend's

house, any woman's house, streetwalker, porch sleeper, and whatever category you can call it, I did it. From Logan, Nicetown, North Philly and other neighborhoods, my night was spent in the later August mist. As long as I had some bud and money in my pocket, I was cool. Amazingly, my belief that continuing school was the only viable option stuck with me. I began hanging out downtown on Chestnut Street with some guys I met randomly. I'd bring oils and incenses to make quick money. As the days went on, Dark, Shorty, Tam and I became real close. They were young boas (guys) that loved to rap and get blazed. Tam was candy hustling. He brought little young dudes from North to make money selling wholesale candy bars for a dollar. Tam had us pumped up to get that candy money. I brought two of my family down and we got paid. The youngsters would go home with cash for looking out. We didn't shortchange them.

The dollar stores in Center City had some good deals on candy bars. For example, you could buy Kit-Kats sometimes three or four for a dollar then sell each bar for a dollar or may be two on the strength of charity. Tam had a family, so he had to bring some dough home every night. For me, it was just about making bud money. I was out on the streets, so it didn't matter.

The weather was nice and I never was broke.

However, I was so irresponsible. Our crew down Center City got so large that you would see over ten dudes just parlaying on the corners of 11th and Market grinding, rapping and hitting on the chicks. We had a good thing going on down there. It opened opportunities to connect with different people such as celebrities, artists, and chicks.

Center City was the stomping grounds for entertainers in town. The club scene was bumping. Sometimes we got in on the strength and other times we had to pay. It was all good until the cops started clamping down on the people hanging around downtown. One day, I stepped off for an errand and left my merchandise and a tape with one of my freestyles on it with the crew. I came back and the cops took my stuff and left a number for me to call. I had some weed in the sack and had to take it as a loss. That demo was gold. The weed amount was small. I wasn't selling at the time but the demo, man.

Lil Shorty still holding down the fort downtown until this day. The women loved him. Brown eyes and swag had them thirsty. Salute. My mom had some friends selling on 11th Street, so they would look out for me as well. The daytime was different from the night. When we scattered, everyone had a home to sleep in except for me. Sometimes, I stayed with Tam for the night, but most of the time, I was scouting out places to lay my head down. My focus remained on my education at CCP (Community College of Philadelphia). Hopefully, I could land a good job and snap out of this nonsense.

Eventually, I was able to transfer to the main campus for the fall semester in 1995. I kept busy writing rhymes in hopes that I could get signed as well. I still linked up with Pone on occasions. He was in school as well. Since my passion was being a disc jockey, I used to hang out with DJ Big Tyme from Olney. He had the skills to wreck shop and I knew his crew from JP. The golden demo that I put down happened to go down in his crib. He told me just freestyle on a track he had put down and mixed Tim Dawg's vocal "Step on my block, ya get beat down" between the intervals. The joint was dope. It took only two times to record it and DJ Big Tyme gave it to me as a present to do what I wanted with it. Some people heard it before it got confiscated. I had the bars and mechanics to make it in the game. The window was closing. I didn't want to be an old rapper nor did my crew.

Po-Po (The police) began raiding downtown and I got picked up on smoking weed down there even though I didn't have any on me. They held me at the local police station on suspicion. They tried to link me to the bag that they were holding. The arresting officer told my crew before this incident that if I wanted that bag I would have to go and claim it and the detective left his card. I forgot that I left my college ID inside with the golden demo tape, bags of bud and my goods in it. The officer in the station said that he has a bag of mines. I told them it wasn't. They said that they would burn the bag if I didn't claim it. I didn't want to get a rap on the intent to deliver because there were about twenty bags of weed in it. I just flat-out denied it and told them to do what they like with it. I got out on ROR and went about my business. I caught up with the crew the next day to smoke some bud.

If things got hot up Market or Chestnut Streets, we would head downwards. Our youngsters would come with us to grind. This time we cut down our numbers to five or six who were true to the game. One brother who I forget his name was our old head. He was the wisest out of us and used to keep us in check particularly Tam. Tam was a bit wild at times. His family was his heart and made sure that he did what he had to do to feed them. Things turned out sour when he found out that his ex-employer was banging his baby's mom. He killed the man and his baby (by accident). The girl survived. Before this altercation, Tam was about hooking up sessions and could spit. He tried to hook us up with Method Man during a time when Meth was in town with Redman doing a show. Meth sold us small timers out.

If you lived in Philly in the 90s, you know that South Street was the joint. You could grind, hang out, network and hit up chicks. I cracked on this short dark skin joint from Jersey while one night and had to make a doctor's visit the next day in Philly. Don't ever get burnt. I hit on another joint down there that was going to Penn State main campus from VA. The young woman was body-handling. I went to visit her on campus for only one reason and she started fronting on me hard. E took the Greyhound for like 6 hours or so thru Harrisburg to get there for an empty invitation. She was welcoming and tried to relax the atmosphere by telling me about herself. Her roommate was away for the weekend. When I pushed up on her, she was like "Wait, let's play some cards." I'm like cool. She pulled out these tarot cards and asked me some questions. I was baffled. Once I refused to play, she got an attitude and played by herself. She kept questioning what's up with me. I told her that I was cool. She knew the real reason of what was bothering me. The next day, she showed me around campus and introduced me to some of her colleagues. No doubt I was ready to roll out. No time for games.

The South Street stories don't end there. I remember the time when my crew and I met the actor Zeus and his wife on South Street. That guy is hilarious. My boyz were yelling "Deebo" from down the street near 4th when he suddenly stopped and looked at us with that Deebo persona and said, "What ya'll looking at my wife for?" We were shaken. Big man smiled and gave us a pound (handshake).

Still, my priority was school. In a few weeks, we would begin the fall semester. I tried to stay close to North Philly as possible, so I could either head up mom's house to shower up or kick it with my boyz downtown. Sometimes, I slept on peoples' porches or in bus stations. Some of the neighbors knew that someone was on their property and turned on the lights. Some even said, "Go ahead man and just guard my crib." Most of the time, I ran away when I heard them coming to the door. Every night was a different scenario.

I tried to get housed over one of my best friend's cribs from childhood that passed away from asthma. The father wasn't trying to hear anything about me staying there for the simple reason that I was Muslim. His wife was sympathetic to me regardless. She'd counsel me for years and made prayer for me every time that I came by to visit. She knew me better than the father. If I had a third mother, it would be her. She was my neighbor's daughter on Carlisle Street back then.

The day I came to her house to ask if I could stay hit the gut. She was down with it, but the dad took the opposite route. He stressed that we are two different beliefs and that I had work to do to change my life. I was pissed, but reality set it that perhaps he was right in a way. Unfortunately, their marriage collapsed after my friend's death. I still gave my condolences and even tried to mend ties with the father, however it never happened. I never experienced this rejection before. I just shook it off and kept moving. Longtime friendships don't mean anything if no one stands up for the truth when confronted.

School is in. Time to clean up my act. With all my registration and books paid for and being on the main campus gave me a new spirit to life. Meanwhile, I just didn't have a place to lay my head at night. Most of my fly gear from my hustling days was with Dew down North. His family got tired of me coming and freshening up at her house that his mom threatened to throw my stuff out. The world was caving in on me. He took my stuff to one smoker who seemed to be trusty. Don't laugh. When I was ready to get my things, this joker said he got rid of it. What a b****! The little stuff that I had up my pop's house wasn't worth getting. It was like breaking into Fort Knox, if my big sister was there.

I lived on the streets through the late summer of 1995 to the mid-fall. The effects of living outside began to show. I'd make sure that I arrived on campus early as 6 AM, so I could wash up in the bathroom before class. I slept on the campus benches for a few nights. One night, one of the security officers had noticed me sleeping out there and offered some words of encouragement. He said that he would open the door early for me to freshen up. I never got a chance to thank him, but if you ever read this book or hear its story, I am grateful for the help.

My first-class (Spanish) began around 7:30 AM. I sat in the front of the teacher off to the side and often nodded off in class. I kept a C throughout the semester. The teacher, who was black, saw my tiresome posture and counseled me after class a few times. I told her of my housing situation and lack of help. She encouraged me to stay in school and do my best to seek a way. A few weeks later, I got a job working as a medical tran-scriber downtown. I lasted only a few weeks and got fired because I appeared to be dozing off asleep at work and smelled like weed.

My friends at CCP didn't know about my housing condition as I kept things under the rug. My crew was larger at CCP (Community College of Philadelphia) than Lincoln University. Some of my closest associates transferred from Lincoln to CCP. We realized that back in Philly: we could work, go to school, get high and still have fun or at least most of us believed so.

We had this one Russian girl named Z who used to hang out with us before class and during breaks. All of us wanted to smash, but she was mad cool. I don't think that she got on. Z was messing around with a Rican boa. Two white friends, R, and J were part of our click, too. They used to love getting high as s***. One morning, they got caught making out in the park up the street from CCP. Most of the time, I'd catch them before school smoking in the park. I'd smoke a little bit. Most of the time, they didn't like to get on with many people. They trusted me and mainly stayed out of the spotlight when it came to the larger sessions.

E was known as the hook-up man for getting-on-sessions on campus that semester. My man Tee, who was with the crew up Lincoln transferred to CCP, bought the liquor, and the crew would all put up for the bud, even Kay (One of my classmates at Central) got on with us. I couldn't imagine that. He was the nerdiest dude in school with a nappy a** afro. He acted goofy and when he laughed, it just didn't sound right. When we linked up in CCP, he was one of my closest boys who I used to bust it up with all the time. He was an art major. The weed brought the abstract out of him. If he could change, I sure could, too.

Campus security was on my a**. It sure reminded me of the movie, Higher Learning. They had my name as the head culprit on campus. I heard this from some of the campus security officers that were cool with me. They tried to pin a big fight on campus on me, but I wasn't even around. Tam was involved though. Tam and Dark used to sometimes come down to hang out when they found out that I was attending CCP. The head of security was like "We know you are the ringleader of this click and we will catch yo ass." He should have known that I'm not the one.

My boyz used to kick it at CCP's quad between classes and after school; freestyling, listening to hip-hop on my radio, and cracking on the ladies. All of my classes ended before 12 PM, so that gave me the whole day to kick it. The weed spots up Girard Avenue were open 24/7. The smoke was always lit.

I finished my classes a bit early and headed up Checkers on Broad and Girard in the rain. I ran into this nursing assistant named A. She was rolling up a blunt in a nurse's uniform while standing under the drive-thru. I'm checking her out and walked over. We both smoked in the rain and exchanged numbers afterward. Homegirl looked so innocent with her pearly eyes and reddish cheeks. She asked me if I were down with another hook-up. You know that E couldn't refuse.

A stayed at the hotel apartments on the corner of 16th and Spring Garden Streets. She told me to bring the herb and call her when I got to the corner. I didn't expect that she lived there. Those apartments were going for at least a grand during those days. She buzzed me in and took me up to the balcony where we smoked and had a little something to drink. Things got a little hot on that balcony and that's all I'm writing on this subject. Somehow, we didn't get a chance to hook-up afterward and saw each other in the Gallery some months later while she was with some of her friends. I should have got the number, man.

———

At CCP, there were too many joints. All my boys were plotting and scheming. Yes, men do gossip. We agreed that none of us were looking for weed head joints even if they were cool as s***. My main man, Mic, from Lincoln attended CCP as well and we hooked up with Dew and Tee. That Lincoln pride followed us around campus.

CCP offered employment opportunities to its students. There was a job posting board on the second floor that I used to check out regularly. I'd scope out if there were any new gigs weekly and found a few promising leads. Some of them were baiting students to come and volunteer and others were serious about offering employment. After checking out the board, I'd usually either head to class or check out my man who had a food cart on the corner and kick it with him for a few minutes before jetting out.

———

On one of those hazy mornings after Spanish class, I received a sincere gut check by two of my older classmates. They noticed that I'd been slipping in class and they must have seen my appearance issues piling up. A sign of poverty among African-Americans that is known is when you haven't groomed in other words "WOLFIN". The seniors asked me to join them for lunch for a talk. Usually, I'd go hang out with the crew or kick it with these Iranian dudes in the cafeteria that used to make me laugh. They usually gossiped about being Shiites and why they were better than Sunnis. I'd join in but only to debate. I had no facts at the time on who was better. That day when I got to the cafeteria, I skipped the Iranians and headed over to the two classmates waiting for me. I took a seat and listened attentively. My heart was humbled by their kindness as they spoke to me about my look in school and the direction I appeared to be heading in. The man had mentioned his experiences dealing with the streets and how he came to know his inner worth. A genuine "There and Now" moment. They recognized that I needed help and I was heedless. As a start, the classmates suggested for me to go to Ridge Avenue Homeless Shelter.

Later that evening, I headed down to Ridge Shelter but got there too late. I was forced to sleep in the streets again. Prancing around near Girard College in the mid-Fall cold, I lit up some bud and canvassed the area. Someone must have seen me wandering aimlessly and called the police. A cop car pulled right up on me and told me that they had a call of a person looking suspicious. As soon as I saw the car, I dropped the blunt. The officer got out the car and ordered me to stop. He searched my pockets and belongings further and questioned me on why I was out in that area. He found a nickel bag of weed and reprimanded me a bit. I told him about my story and about the shelter being closed. He offered to help me by driving me there and checking me in at the desk. If the officer did that, then imagine the power, they have to change the society positively. The shelter staff lets me in with no issues and I thanked the officer. He made sure that I got rid of the weed before we got to the shelter.

I had a bed to rest in for the night at least. It wasn't as dirty as I thought. The showers were clean and the staff was friendly. The cot was comfortable and the men kept to themselves. As long as I got back in by 7 PM, I could get a bed, a meal, and a hot shower. After school, I'd play the streets a bit and made sure that I got back in time. I was at Ridge for three nights until they transferred me to a shelter inside a church on Chelten and Ogontz Avenues.

At the new shelter, I was processed and was informed that there was a fifteen-day blackout for all new incoming residents. I told them that I was a student at CCP. At the time, I wasn't employed. They gave me until 5 PM to report in. The purpose of the blackout is to stop you from using drugs. That wasn't my agenda, according to the belief that marijuana is natural and grown on Earth.

A person staying at any shelter meant that they

would be randomly drug tested. My first drug test proved so. A counselor named Mr. Lon said that he would give me one chance only. The temperature was getting colder as we were heading to late November 1996. I didn't need any other proof except the cold. The weed wasn't worth it.

The snow had begun to come down and it reached at least thirty-three inches in our area. I complied with the program rules and began trying to reform myself. One of the evening staff members had brought a Super Nintendo to the job, so we used to play NBA Live '95 and we would split the matches most of the time. I found some Muslim brothers like Nafis, Yousef and others in the shelter as well. We talked about the deen and everyone had a story. I was one of the youngest dudes in the joint and the old heads looked out.

Everyone had a cigarette habit. If you had Newties (Newports), the guys would hit you up right away. The men lived separate from the women and several of the guys had spouses and children in the women's shelter at another location. I wasn't looking for love in the shelter. One of the cooking staff members wanted me so badly. A big boned dark-skinned thick joint with a big a**. Let me stop. She'd call me down to the basement to help her get supplies just to seduce me. I was shocked. The woman was cute and all, but at least twenty-five years older than me. I think she had a child my age. The lady did hook a brother up with some stuff. Too bad, it wasn't the right stuff.

The whole deal of staying at the shelter was better than being out there in the cold. Some people insisted on living out in the street. Not me. There was a Muslim brother who was seventeen staying at the shelter. I was puzzled on how he got up here but never asked him what was his situation. Another guy I met said that he was a gigolo at night and that people would pick him on the corners in downtown Center City. He told me how doctors including male ones used to pay him big money to eat the gun. I shaked my head when he told me that he wasn't gay.

There was chapel service a few times a week. I opted not to attend. No one pressured the people to come, however, if there was NA meeting inside, you had to attend. I didn't consider myself an addict, so what's the point of going. Management gave me some leeway and I was grateful.

I enjoyed the good times at that shelter, too. A group of us played football at night in the deep snow one evening. I scored a few touchdowns playing wide receiver that match. Even some of the staff joined in.

Within the shelter, most rooms were doubles or quads. I got in a double with my roommate, Rich, from

Southwest Philadelphia. He used to always rap about his wife and kids and often used the pay phone to phone home. He would come back to the room with a smile on his face after talking to them. Rich was trying to get his life together by staying in the shelter and away from Southwest. The drug scene in Southwest Philly was an endemic. We had a disagreement once but made up. All of us had some issues that we were dealing with. No one wanted to stay at that shelter long-term except for the goalless.

It was a fortune being single without kids. I used to sympathize with Rich even when he was stressed out. The pressure of being away from the family can kill the morale. Rich left the shelter shortly after we made up. I believed he moved in with his girlfriend and kids back down Southwest. I hope for him the best.

Meanwhile, I had the room to myself and that was the beginning of a major problem. Some dudes became jealous. That wasn't a big deal. However, there was a dude from the Stenton Park area of Logan who tried to get a little too close. I remember seeing him play ball at the park when he was younger and straight. Dude could ball back then. I used to say what's up when passing by him in the shelter just on the strength of us being from the same hood. I spoke and kept it moving. He thought that because I spoke that it meant that I liked him or something. He happened to take it further and tried to come at me on one occasion.

He came by my room when I had the door open and said that he had a problem with his TV. I offered to fix it, when we got to his room, he suddenly closed the door and locked it while I was checking out the TV. I turned around and he tried to grip me up from behind. You know ya boy E was having none of that. I was ready to put his a** in the hospital but I thought about the repercussions; not getting permanent housing if I got kicked out. Fighting was against the rules and warranted immediate dismissal. Upset and in shock, I reported it to the staff right away. Mr. Lon called us down to his office and warned that guy about his offence and gave him one chance. He was ordered to apologize and we went about our business. I knew it was almost time to move on from the shelter.

Still, at CCP, I started job-hunting on the board upstairs more seriously. I had to get out of the shelter. MCC (Maternity Care Coalition) had interviewed me and they gave me a gig almost a week after the interview. Now I can begin putting money aside to start my exit plan from the shelter. We got paid biweekly and after my first paycheck, I needed a vacation especially after that incident. I put in a request to the shelter to travel to Baltimore Harbor for the weekend. They made me promise not to use any drugs or get into any trouble while I was away. I agreed and permission was granted.

I rode down Baltimore on Greyhound and rented a hotel room for one night or two on Baltimore Harbor. The room was cozy and loaded with alcohol in the fridge and a big screen TV. It cost around $139 for the night. I didn't have all of my identification with me but was still able to get it after talking a little to the desk employee. Most of the time, I went outside to chill on the Harbor looking for the chicks.

Inside, E stayed looking out the window into the Harbor. My life was steadily changing for the better. I was clean and disciplined. This was Olympic year "1996". Why not celebrate by getting something? I headed to the Swatch Shop on the Harbor and copped me this fly Swatch Olympic classic watch that lit up blue when you press the button on the side. The joint was fly. I don't think that I bought another watch after that one. Time's up and now E got to go back to Philly.

One of my biggest challenges now was facing my old colleagues who were still getting on. I'm working and forced to stay clean. The winter of 1997 semester was in effect. My male friends at CCP were shocked to see that I gave up getting high. The ladies were even more shocked. They remembered me as the weed-head maniac. The one, who set up the sessions and made sure they went through to the end. I had all my colleagues' class schedules to the tee when I was getting high. Now, the women were like damn boy you look so good. Even the Russian joint was giving me some airtime. I think she broke up with her boyfriend. We talked a few times on the phone. Meanwhile, I was hauling in digits like the phone companies.

My former weed habits transformed into shopping extravaganzas. I'd hit up Cheltenham Mall, The Gallery, King of Prussia Mall and Center City for the latest fresh gear. There was a time that I went all-out and got me some white and black gator sneaker boots, rocked them with some black sweatpants and a matching paisley shirt. People were like damn bro, you hit them hard. I wore that outfit once and that was it. Just too flashy for a bro.

Things began turning around for me in that six-month period while I was staying at the shelter on Ogontz Avenue. No one from my click knew that I stayed in a shelter not even Pone. Sometimes, people would ask me where I lived, but I'd be like with one of my friends. As far as the ladies, I'd meet them at their houses. I went to basketball games with them and etc.

The weather began to break. I was faced with a big decision about where to live next. Karim, who was in charge of the transfers, tried to shift me to a stricter facility where I would have to come in at 3 PM and you could only seek home passes on the weekends picked in a pool. Karim was Muslim and looked out for the brothers for different community services. He told me that was the only alternative on the table if I wanted to continue in the program. The goal was to stay in the system long enough into order to get transitional housing. These programs varied in degrees of strictness. I told him that I would leave the program and find my own spot. I was given thirty days to do so. OSHA returned my money collected from my savings at work with no problems.

I searched the classifieds in the Daily News and found a shared room in a three-story house in East Mount Airy around the corner from Germantown and Gorgas Lane. The location was good as well as the property because it was near the 23 Bus and the room was the closest to the bathroom. *I had a neighbor who kept the noise going all nightlong. She was fighting with her boyfriend all nightlong. She was playing her music all nightlong.* Dammit. Once the roaches came and the complaints grew about that neighbor, the landlord put his foot down, got rid of the disruptive tenant and her boyfriend, cleaned the house and painted it. The new tenants were much better although there were still some instances of disruption, especially on the first floor.

My daily schedule was class in the morning, work afterward until 4 PM, and then come home around about 5 PM and go jogging. I had still had to get my weed on, no doubt. Sometimes, my neighbor V used to come by to chill and watch a movie or two with her kids and I. She lived next door with her mother and two children. There was an attraction between us, but we were real tight. She came by the room one evening after I finished showering to watch a movie. I was all olive-oiled up in my briefs, lying on the bed in the dark. Most of the time, she just walked right in after a little knock. She sat on the bed looking at me all puzzled while I was smoking a J. I knew what she wanted to do but we just talked and she left. V told me a few days later how she felt about our friendship, that night and us. It was too precious to f*** up. I respected that. One of the first times that I realize that men and women can be friends without banging but it's a dangerous playing field. Eventually, she found love and she seemed content.

In my journeys downtown, I met this young jawn from Upper Darby on Chestnut Street while I visiting my man Dew. Shorty was light brown skinned, tight and athletic. Scoping her walking down the street with her bicycle, I had to crack on her. She seemed open-minded and we went back to Dew's crib on Chestnut Street. Dew stepped off and went to the Gallery. After thirty minutes or so, Shorty began passing out on me. I was scared to death. I carried her to the bathroom and put water on her face and that beautiful body. She woke back up kissing me. I'm like, "What in the world just happened?" My man Dew came back some time later and I told him what had happened. I whispered to her, "Was it me?" She said that she had low blood pressure.

We giggled and snuggled up watching the Pittsburgh Steelers play with Dew for a bit and then headed out for pizza. She was ready to go back home in Upper Darby. I offered to pay for her to get back (like a gentleman) and she said that she would cycle back. We kept in touch daily and eventually became good mates. I met her mother and a few of her siblings at her crib in Upper Darby and they were glad for her to meet someone who cared regardless of our age difference, which was a year or two only. There was something special about her. She was quiet, bad as ****, introverted and definitely my type. She came by the crib in Mount Airy a few times to hang out with me. When she told me that she was moving to Virginia for some mental related issues or something, our relationship slowly phased out. I was sad that we lost contact.

Around the house where I was staying, the test with the women started intensifying. This light-skinned old head joint with long black hair with hazel eyes kept hitting on me when no one was around. She looked good as crap and had a man. I questioned her about why does she want me. You know where that was going. Whenever I was down in the kitchen and we were alone, she'd started her s***. I played along to the tune, but I never got in because she moved out a few weeks later.

Across the hall from her was another dark-skinned slim jawn who was a nurse. She made passes at me as well but didn't have a man. She was a straight up freak, bro. I could sense her coming down the hall. She had this aroma that was so enticing that it would have you in a trance. One time I passed by her and said something fly to her. She told me to come upstairs and let's talk about it. I got upstairs and it was done even as she was talking on the phone. This joint would come by room almost every morning around 6 just before I went to work. E was taken, hostage.

Every morning, I'm rushing to work because of her. I told her we had to slow down. She was begging me, please daddy. I felt so compelled. My resistance began to kick in and I told her one more time and that's it. You know how that is. A few days later, I caught one of my neighbors across the street up in her room looking like he was about to smash. I was done. That's the end. I saw her a few years later passing by Makkah Market. We hugged and the urge was still there.

There was a woman living on the corner up the street from me who was bodied out and I had to have her. I cracked on her on way coming up Musgrave Street and she gave me the digits. When we finally hooked up, she told me that she had a man living with her who kept tabs on her. Her time away from him was her time to do what she wanted. She was a social drinker and love to smoke cigarettes. One time she came through high as crap, I took her upstairs and boy it was over. Her body was mad crazy. She came through a few more times and we parted ways when I refused to give her cigarettes one evening. Any excuse to cover it up, I guess.

Why these women keep hitting on me, left and right? There was an intern, who I didn't even know lived right up the street from me at the gig and came by my spot later that evening to smoke some bud and made me pay. The next day at work, I felt so guilty. I'm like what in the world is happening. A Muslim joint with a daughter tried to hit on me a few blocks away from the pad. I got to do something about this.

I began to exercise even more to keep my physical activity even though I was still smoking. The bud seemed like it gave me that extra boost. I loved the vibe of Mount Airy and still do. I began to realize that I needed to get my s*** together.

You may ask how this guy became Muslim. Here's the history on it:

My story about Islam and becoming one started when I attended Sister Clara Muhammad's Mosque in West Philadelphia for a prayer. I had the urge to go there before accepting Islam to see how it was. I chose one Friday to go down there and then visit my grandparents who lived off 42nd and 43rd and Haverford. Following with the faithful there as if I was Muslim, I listened attentively to the sermon by the Imam Shamsuddin Ali (one of the religious leaders in Philly then). It was different from being in church. There was a tranquil vibe to the whole ceremony. Comrades were hugging one another afterward and shaking hands with everyone. This harmony was genuine. I decided the following week to declare my faith in

Islam and arrived early to do so. After the Friday sermon, I walked up to the Imam and saw my man Shaheed from the Yunk in the front row. I'm like," Bro, I didn't know you were Muslim?" He said, "Yeah, man and some Arabic words". I told him I was there to take my shahada (faith declaration). He said, "Let's do it." Now, that it's done. The path of knowledge and clarity of purpose got easier. Let's talk a little bit more about my job at MCC.

My supervisor named K at MCC was a really nice woman. She was an Irishwoman who was sentimental, understanding and even joked with us on many occasions to keep the mood at the office lively. Ms. Carmen, who was the secretary of the office, also was cool and down to earth. We used to order lunch together a couple times a week. The office staff knew I was Muslim and it wasn't ever an issue. I came to work on time and did my job professionally and whatever happened outside after work was nobody's business. There were outreach coordinators in the back of the office who I used to talk to as well such as Ms. P and Ms. Dee. Ms. P and I was from the same neighborhood in fact. We talked a lot. She had three kids and was looking for the right man. With those bubbly brown eyes and slim figure, old head was nice. She'd made passes at me. I used to spit fly stuff to her and even came by the crib but we knew that nothing come happen between us because of the age difference. Her oldest daughter was a few years younger than me and it would have been a nightmare if we hooked up. Ms. Dee used to crack jokes at her desk just to pass time. I was the only man in the office, so the women used to take their expressive shots at me. It was cool.

During lunch, I'd often go to the Free Library on 20th and Vine Streets. Walking pass the old Court-house on 1801 Vine Street for juvenile offender brought back some crazy memories of my time spent in the system as an adolescent. E is a new man in a new direction. My gusto was the money, ladies, rap music, and the weed. I couldn't imagine life with them. As long as I stayed in school, came to work on time and sober, and paid my bills off, I believed that it would pay off one day.

———

A few months into the gig and around my last semester at CCP, I met a Muslim brother named Ed, who was working as a social worker for another company. There was a scheduled meeting with our organization and others at MCC. I first saw him in the bathroom and thought the brother was praying inside it. He was making wudu (ablution) and I saw his prayer rug near his belongings on the floor. I gave him the greetings and we became good friends and family for life.

I started going to Friday prayers regularly and prayed as much as I could. My daily prayers weren't consistent in the beginning between two, three, or four and sometimes five. I still had those other skeletons in my closet if you know what I mean. At the house on Musgrave, a Muslim brother had moved downstairs on the first floor. He had a temper, but was good peoples. We talked about Islam and he told me about Masjidullah on Ogontz Avenue. He gave me my first Islamic garment to wear; a burgundy Pakistani matching shirt and pants set. He would attend Friday prayers down UMM masjid in South Philly. We never attended the prayers together, but I began going up there hoping for some direction in my life.

E THAT MUSLIM GUY

I first heard about the G aka Germantown Masjid from as far back as 1995. I even attended some of the Friday sermons with my man Emil from my stomping grounds known as Nicetown. We got close in my latter teenage years. Usually, we met up at Stenton Park to get on and kick it around the hood. When we both discovered Islam, we became tighter. I remember in 1995, the G used to be so crowded for Jumah prayer that you would have to sit in the imam's office to hear the sermon. During the week after work in 1997, I'd try to head to the G for Fajr (morning prayer) catching the 23 bus down from Gorgas Lane. The other prayers if I could get them in on time, I'd head to Masjidullah. Every Sunday at the masjid, there was a morning Quranic class around 10 AM and after Zuhr (noon prayer), the imam held an open topic of discussion with the community. I was digging the Quran class because the children were memorizing Quran and it was beautiful. I learned Surah Al-Maun (Chapter 108 in the Quran) with them.

As I started regularly attending Masjidullah, I saw one of my friend's mothers from Central there for some classes named Ms. Dee. We began speaking often on the phone and she was so happy that I became Muslim. I didn't know that Ms. Dee, Kha (my friend from Central), and the rest of their immediate family were attending that masjid. I remember listening to Masjidullah tapes at their house when I came by. Abdul Aleem's (the former imam) sermons and lectures were informative and practical. He talked about Islam being your life system and ordering it in your lifestyle. The imam had graduated from Duke and seemed to be on point when he talked about Islamic life. As my faith grew, I started to connect with other colleagues at other masjids as well.

One of the first friends I met up the G (Germantown Masjid) was Abdul Hakim, who used to come up to Masjidullah for Fajr prayer sometimes. We used to talk after the prayer on many occasion until the sun had risen. Our conversations centered on faith, supplications, and some daily events. We always reminded each other to say "Subhanallah wa bi hamdihi" which means [Glory be to Allah and with his praise alone] 100 times a day sin order to get the reward of one thousand good deeds and removal of a thousand bad deeds. It seemed like if we didn't say it for that day, then our days would feel incomplete.

As Hakim and I grew in friendship, the more we realized that we were missing something by going to that masjid. Germantown Masjid had the learning materials, teachers, callers and information that Masjidullah did not. The problem with the G was there were individuals down there always criticizing people and acting all hardcore. Sometimes, I'd ride past the Masjid on the 23 bus and view what was going on.

It was a movement going on up there and the brothers were serious about putting their message out in the community. These brothers walking up and down the street with big beards, high waters, and Islamic paraphernalia. The sisters were in all black with their faces covered. Up the street from Germantown Masjid was a place called the Dawah Center where all the brothers used to get together and sell tapes, clothes, and other Islamic items. Inside the masjid, there would be rows of brothers praying, making supplication and reading Quran. Some even had their arms all the way up while invocating. I was amazed by their devotion. The imam made sure the lines were straight with no gaps and checked them all the way to the last line. Once in a while, my foot would get crushed by one who was excessively zealous. The Muslims take their religion seriously up there.

I formed a working relationship with the Imam of the community and was offered a job to work at the grocery store up the street. As long as I was close to the masjid to get some of that knowledge, it was perfect for me. This job came about when the new office manager at MCC had ended my employment because of my religion.

Ms. K (the office manager of two years) had left MCC for a better position. A new office manager was hired; an African-American woman who was cool in the beginning. She talked about her love for the church all the time. As she got familiar with her role and the staff, she began showing her true colors by making comments to me that signaled that against Islam. At first, I laughed off her comments and focused on work. A few weeks later, another African-American guy named E got hired. We were the only two men in the office. The brother and I used to go and pray together and she would criticize us for taking too many breaks. We only prayed twice maximum during work hours. Anyway, she called me in one morning and said, "This isn't going to work out between us, so I will have let you go. I shook my head in disbelief. She was so blatant in her hate for Islam. The CEO didn't say anything and that was a bad thing. I never had a problem with anyone at the company. It is what it is.

———

Around the time that I was at MCC, I started a new hustle from a brother that I call Uncle. He was a baker and his cakes were the bomb. Everyone in the city knows Uncle. I arrived in the late 90s and his cake business was taking off. I'd go to his house after school when he was living in West Philly to get some banana nut, carrot, and other kinds of cakes, bring them down Center City, school, wherever and off them joints with the quickness especially at that park on 19th and Walnut. I would prop my basket up with the slices and people would come and buy em' up. The good thing about selling those cakes is that I never ate them nor liked them.

I needed a place that was bigger and more secluded. Went to a few places but end up getting a one-bedroom apartment in the Olney section of Philly right on Roosevelt Boulevard. My little French lemon got me around the city and school giving me problems almost weekly. My new landlord was Native American and stayed on the bottom he house was a duplex. I lived on the second floor and had my own entrance. A few times a week, I'd come down to the landlord's place and visit him. He'd give me advice on life and etc. Afterward all changed when I did something that he seemed not to agree with. We will talk about this later.

As I began practicing Islam, I noticed that Muslims put emphasis on family and getting married. All the faithful around the masjid were talking about whom they wanted to get married or whom the others were married to. This had me consistently thinking about marriage in my last semester of college. E and the ladies, as you already know.

My schedule was full. I had class in the early morning, class again midday, hit up the G for work in the afternoon to early evening, and grind my cakes downtown or be at the masjid. If possible, I'd get back home after the Isha (early night prayer).

At school, my whole persona had changed. My colleagues couldn't believe it. I still hung out with them in the morning except that I wasn't puffin anymore. What's up with that? I was on that natural high. The women were clocking me even harder than before. E was fresh, casually dressed, and groomed with that gold tee. That Russian chick finally tried to come at me when she dumped the Rican boa. I remember that boa was crazy. He picked her up after school and never got out of his car. We talked on the phone a few times but nothing happened. I remember her hugging me when she saw me and sitting on my lap sometimes in the quad. That booty was right. People thought I was hitting it but I wasn't. I liked her, but follow-ups weren't my style.

My thing was the Muslima (Muslim woman). She was the one who could help me grow. While working at the imam's store, there were a few prospects to consider. There were also two factions up the G at the time heading in opposite directions. There were the casual Muslim brothers and sisters who just came to pray and didn't get into the mix of whom was on it or off it. At first, I was from them. The second faction was the zealous Muslim brothers who took their time trying to knick-pick every single infraction that they came across. If you didn't look like them and talk like them, then you were not on it. I felt uneasy being at the store at times and having to hear from some of those guys about why I dress a certain way and who do I follow. My job was only to come in and manage the store. Both factions had their positives and negatives. I wasn't trying to get into those political or religious issues. My knowledge was limited. On one side, you had brothers who wanted to run the masjid and run their businesses as well and the other side who were strictly trying to take the masjid on the theory the other side were not doing their job good enough. I stayed out of it. When Hakim and I spoke on the matter, we agreed the knowledge had to precede the politics even if it was in favor of the youngsters trying to take over the masjid.

There was much friction going on at the G in 1997 unlike when I first visited back in '95. I decided to go to other masjids throughout the city as well. I got tired of the gossip around removing the imam and the acting administration at the G, disassociating anyone who wasn't on the dawah, and etc. In 1997, my concerns were school and trying to learn more about Islam than getting into that chaos. I begin praying at a masjid called Masjid Salafiyah on 27th and Oxford Streets most of the time because the Friday prayers were early and close enough to get to after my Friday morning class. Meanwhile, I was interested in MSA at CCP and spoke with its members about joining. I'm not sure if I ever joined.

———

Community College of Philadelphia had Friday

prayers as well. I started attending them regularly, too. The imam, Abdul Hafiz used to give the khutbah (Friday sermon) as well as Br. Abu Sumayyah and others (may Allah preserve them all). I began taking from him realizing that he knew exactly how to connect with people on their understanding. The khutbahs used to be so informative and straightforward. I'd ask him questions after the sermon about books and other matters and he would give me the real.

Praying at Masjid Salafiyah, Germantown, Ridge Avenue and at CCP gave me a chance to hear more about the Dawah Salafiyah (the way of the pious predecessors in Islam). When I prayed at Masjid Salafiyah back in 97, Imam Abdul Matin, and Abu Sumayyah usually led the Friday prayers along by Hafiz. The sermons were fire. The brothers in that community were warmhearted and weren't caught up in the issues uptown. Sometimes after Jumah, I'd go to Ridge Avenue to catch the Friday sermon as well. Sometimes, I could catch both sermons. Just needed the remembrance.

I recall now that while I was at CCP also taking part in events hosted by the Muslim Students' Association or known as MSA. One memorable event happened to be in collaboration with Temple University's MSA to host one the first annual Muslim Conference at Temple's main campus. The guest speakers were Dr. Khalid Blankenship, Anwar and Anas Muhaymin and well as others. They gave talks on various topics and had the crowd upbeat. In the vending area, I ran into some of the brothers from up the Dawah Center. They were selling books, clothes and other Islam paraphernalia. The brothers always had informative materials and tapes. The biggest issue for most of us who didn't regularly attend the G was how harsh some of those brothers were to those who didn't show their faces up there often. Knick-picking at every single infraction they could find on you or in you turned many away from the masjid. The constant reminder about your pants below your ankle being in the hellfire, barefaced men resembling women, not wearing Arabian garments, taking from the wrong people was irking. I accepted the information as well as my man, Hakim but give us a damn chance to come around.

I wasn't into that. I just wanted to be around the Muslims and learn the deen (religion). Some of the associates that I befriended up the G were against this knick-picking as well. It even got to one of my colleagues. A group of them told him the meat and chicken sold at the supermarket where he worked aren't halal (permissible for Muslims), so he can't work there. There were a few Muslim butchers in our city like Imam AA market on Susquehanna Avenue, some Arabs down Masjid Al-Aqsa, Chicken Hut and Makkah Market slaughtering, but for those who lived in remote parts of the city and didn't drive, it was difficult to come by or couldn't afford it. Yes, I'm calling out the butchers. The prices were outrageous compared with the local supermarkets. Some brothers and sisters, who publicly chastised anyone who ate from the local supermarkets, secretly went to the local supermarkets to buy chicken, beef, lamb, and goat. They got clowned if found doing so. I know a brother that even left the G over this issue and never came back. Anyway, the scholars explained the position clearly and even showed us by eating at the restaurants in our city that were Christian-slaughtered. Still, some of the community up the G was insistent about only eating the halal meat.

Man, I remember around 97, a halal restaurant off Champlost and Old York Road that all the brothers used to eat at. They used to serve the best platters uptown until they closed down. No, I didn't forget Halal Bilal. Me, Hakim, and another stocky bro used to head down Champlost all the time after Isha. I think that our stocky friend used to work there afterwards before they closed down. There was a cute sister working there as well. The boys would try to hit on her and make excuses why to go up there and eat after salaat.

The friction between the administration at the masjid and the Dawah Center was intensifying. Meetings were held inside the masjid, guns were about to be drawn, hurtful words were hurled at one another and many neutral people began leaving the G to get away from the fitnah (troubles). "Let the Sunnah go forth and don't stop it" was the motto. Brothers from East Orange and other East Coast cities joined in which made things even more interesting. I cried at one of the meetings and told the brothers to get their acts together.

It even got to the point the current masjid administration locked the doors of the masjid for a day or two. That was the turning point. The people, who were sympathetic to the imam looked at it as an act unwarranted. The doors reopened and that gave impetus to the colleagues on the side of the Dawah As-Salafiya. Within the next few weeks, the momentum shifted drastically for the Dawah Center's lead becoming the new administration and eventually that's what took place. The imam signed the lease to the building or forcibly had done so depending on what side you believed. The old administration members started going to other masjids and started one on Broad Street. The Dawah Center and its associates began to change the course of the masjid to what it is today as the lead masjid in the United States in calling to the way of the Pious Predecessors known as the As-Salaf As-Salih. The doors are open for whoever would embrace the way of the Salaf and whoever had an issue weren't welcomed. Honestly, I was in the middle because on one hand, I was cool with the former administration, employed by them and liked their approach and how they raised their kids and on another hand, I felt the younger brothers had some truth to what they were preaching and it made sense regardless of their character flaws in delivery. As Hakim used to mention that we had to roll with the truth even though many those brothers who were calling to it were hard-core and of bitter character.

Right before the time of the overthrow or takeover depending on whose side you were on, I had my first chance of courtship with one of the administrative leaders' daughter of the masjid. The story goes as the following:

A middle-aged brother had seen me come into the masjid regularly and on this particular day around

Zuhr (Noon), sat and had a chat with me as we waited for the adhan (Call for prayer) for prayer. We've chatted before and he knew that I had just finished college and working at the store up the street for his friends. I believe that he was a partner in the business as well. The brother asked me if I were interested in getting married and replied in a nonchalant manner of yes, meaning "hell yeah". I wanted to take that next step in deen (religion). It's half of your religion to get married. A bro was all for the halal skins as some refer to it. Most importantly, a brother needs a good sister to start a family. The brother invited me to his house somewhere in South Jersey to talk to him more about the sister and to meet her other family members. It turned out to be more like a get-together because some of the sons of the brothers that were part of the administration also attended. The bro A for short, who memorized the entire Quran and led the prayers up the G if he was present, was there. All the faithful had a love for him because we were witnesses during the process of him becoming the first African-American to memorize the Quran in America. He did it and everyone up the G and the other masjids, was proud of him. *What an achievement!*

Back to the story, I met the mother, the sister (who I was interested in), and her stepfather who happened to be the brother in the living room of their vast home. I didn't know the brother was the stepfather. It seems that we had made some progress and intents were placed. Sis had it going on both ways however, it was up to the father back in Philly to give permission for his daughter to get married. After the Jersey trip, I got in touch with the father and met him one Friday at Jumah at Quba Institute in West Philly. Quba Institute was a unique place to be. It was a place known for people trying to memorize the Quran, but you had much mingling going on there as well. Who am I to talk? I have to keep things 100 with you.

The G was the total opposite. If the husband and wife were talking in the front, it looked strange. Anyway, when I met the sister's father, we meshed well and set up a dinner date at Red Lobster in the Northeast, so we can get to know each other. The date was set and I was looking forward to it. I spoke with the sister a few times on the phone before the dinner date and it was a go.

I didn't tell any of my friends at the masjid about what was going on. The talk of deviance was common like the flu up there. A few days before I was scheduled to meet with the sister and father, my car started giving me a lot more trouble than before. My brakes were slow to respond, so I had taken it to the shop in Logan where one of the brothers from up the G recommended me to get the problem fixed. The mechanic told me the brakes needed padding or something and not to worry even if it felt like they didn't respond quick enough, they just need some air in them. I had confidence in him on the strength that he fixed my car a few times before without any issues.

The day of the big date arrived and I was on my way to Quba to pick up the sister and her father when my car brakes worsen. I downplayed the incident when I told the father about it. He said, "You, two, drive in Eric's car and I will follow right behind you." In the back of my mind thinking, "I'm saying sir, we might have some issues here." I was ready to decline driving, but out of pride, I didn't want to mess up the date by driving with the father. Once the sister and I got on Roosevelt Boulevard near Hunting Park, I noticed that my brakes went out on me. I made a detour on the exit closest to my home in Olney.

———

Al-Hamdulilah (All praises due to Allah), there was a green light at every corner after the exit on the expressway. I'd take my foot off the gas, slow down and turn fittingly. I told the sister about a block before we got to the backstreet of my house what was going on. She flipped out as expected. With only one block to go, I made a quick right almost having to stop at the red light. To park, I rear-ended the car parked in front of me. My emergency brake had even stopped working. SABOTAGED. She jumped out the car, angered and scared, running to her father. I explained the situation of my car and that I had taken it to the shop a day ago to get fixed. He said, "Don't worry about it, we can take my car."

I never recovered from that night with that sister and even though we had a nice dinner, she was shaken up the whole time about that car incident. The father called me and told me that his daughter wouldn't be interested. I was sad, but there was nothing I could do. I ran into the sister a year later up Fern Rock and she told me that she had gotten married. It is what it is.

———

E started attending the G (Germantown Masjid) on a full-time basis now the smoke had cleared with the coup d'état. I didn't live too far away nor did I live close by, but not having that French lemon now made things more difficult. I wasn't interested in getting another car because that lemon had me forking out money weekly. I got tired of going to Girard Avenue for parts and bringing them to the mechanic to fix this piece of s***. Yeah, I'd never buy a French car again and I said it.

Back on Septa, coming from the Boulevard and surprisingly it took the same time to get to my destinations as if I were driving. The bus stop was outside the front of my house and they ran often. The money that I put out for a weekly transpass was far less than I had put out for gas, oil, and repairs for the French Lemon.

The little grocery store owned by the old administration had closed down once the G fell out their hands. There was another opportunity for marriage with a sister I worked with, but I declined. She winded up marrying my man Akh, who I hung out with when I was 14 and got locked up with. To this day, I believe they are still married and have children. May Allah preserve them, Ameen. Akh was my man from up B & O. I shared our moments earlier in the series.

The more I attended the G, the more my physical appearance began to change as well such as dress, growing the beard, and the G-Town lingo. I went thru a new change in my life that I never expected. I was never a follower and had to keep an open mind even though my life was adapting to the new surroundings. I remember there being about three or four masjids in our city that were following the Dawah As-Salafiya in the late 90s. If I didn't pray at the G, then I'd probably be at the other Salafi masjids especially Ridge Avenue because my mother stays in the same neighborhood.

After salat (prayer), I'd go to her house to try to recover my Sega Genesis that she had taken away in 1995 from me to no use. I winded up finding it at a neighbor's house down the street while I was looking for one of my younger brothers in 1997. Two years later, I was still pissed off.

I liked Ridge Avenue masjid. The vibe of the brothers and sisters there was much different from the G. The masjid was in the heart of the ghetto and its members were down to earth. That impressed me so much that I tried to attend prayers as often as I could, often driving there when I had the car to catch the prayers. My man, Dew from Lincoln University accepted Islam and was going there often and had married at the masjid as well. After our business venture went sour as mentioned in Volume Two, we remained good friends. He started selling goods on the corner of 29th and Ridge. I'd come to hang out with him and his family a few times a week. They were happy together. I was glad my man finally hit a home run.

Dew is a deep dude and an inspiration to me. There aren't too many deep friends that I've come across in my life like Dew. We lived the dorm life, its apathies and great times. We crossed paths back at CCP, was business partners, and now we are Muslims. I look at him as one of my greatest friends to this day even though we haven't seen each other physically in years.

Seeing him and his family happy made me happy. Of course, those questions of when are you getting married started bearing down on me. I was for it as long haul as long as the sister was good and pious. One sister had hung out with his wife and was single. They tried to hook me up. My street senses told me no for one simple reason, North Philly. Dew and his wife told me the sister is deenin (practicing accordingly). One time, the sister came thru, carrying an Islamic book, looking all good and wearing a black khimar (head covering) and black overgarment. I screamed to myself that it's on. Was it a trap or did it work out? You'll hear about it in the next chapter.

THAT MARRIAGE LIFE AND BEING A STUDENT

CHAPTER THIRTEEN

Let us break the ice a bit. I thought that getting my associates degree, having a car, a job, and a few other side hustles would be enough to start exploring marriage in Islam. I grew tired of the temporary relationships throughout the years and party life. Someday there would be Mrs. Reese, but who could it be. The opportunity that Dew had posed to me seemed practicable. Anything coming from him and my closest companions, I would consider it. Dew always used to advise me in matters. He would be like Cee (My nickname from college), "We need to set up something for our seeds." That term rings a bell in my head even now as we speak. Life decisions separate men from boys.

The sister was from North. I broke my genuine rule not to f*** with girls from down there. Time to put aside my past codes and consider Islam as being my criterion. If it would not have worked out, I could at least fall back on what Islam dictated and not the rules of the street. Whenever I met her, she was shy and bashful. The girl had a nice smile and some swagger to her. When I met her guardian, he encouraged me to look at the benefits of getting married and held high praise for the sister. I was new in Islam, he advised me to take into retrospect the fact that this was a matter of maturity. He advised the sister with the same.

Being away from my parents and living on my own had given me a sense of maturity but perhaps not enough. I was lonely although I acted like I was not. The property owner was lonely, too, and often chatting for long periods at a time rumbling as if he was in therapeutic session. I would have to excuse myself abruptly. This brother needs some excitement in his life. If I marry this woman, it would award me with that opportunity.

She was young in her last year of high school, beautiful, and had it going on for herself. I am not blasting North Philly because I was born down North, but if you are from my city, you would know exactly what I mean when I say what I say. Different neighborhoods in every city have different attitudes and characteristics. The point is that everyone knows the what, where, who, and why you should or should not in our city. It is the code of the streets everywhere.

Back to the story, there was an Islamic function at Al Aqsa Masjid on 4th Street when I met this sister and talked to her for the first time. My big brother, Dawood, who passed away some years ago, saw me creeping and talking to the sister outside the masjid with Dew and his peoples. He called out to me and said that I should get with the sister if I were serious. He must have seen the stars in my eyes. I still remember the look on his face. I had been to Al Aqsa a few times and had some good friends who attended that masjid. The sister was dressed so nice in that black garb that I could not stop staring at her.

A few weeks later, I was ready to do the marriage, so I went to the guardian to express my intent fully. A few days before that marriage date, I had met with the sister's mother and siblings in some rundown work shoes. I was just getting off and the sister took notice of my shoes and laughed. It was unexpected because the guardian told me to meet him straight after work at the butcher shop. Once we got inside the sister's house, her mother quizzed me on why I wanted to marry her daughter so young. I replied for the religion only. Her mother wasn't Muslim but seemed down if her daughter was. My parents did not understand why I was doing it either.

My teenage years were not that long ago. At the sit-down, it felt like it. We planned the date after the meeting. A few nights later, I came up with the dowry and we had gotten married after I got off work. It was not the traditional wedding format as known in the West culture and much simpler. Dew drove us back to my apartment on the Boulevard afterward. The bride and I held hands in the back of the car and seemed destined for the stars.

The first few weeks were the best. I'd pick her up from school in the evening after work. Once we got home, she would cook a meal that would put me on the floor. We would chat the night away about things that African-Americans gossip about. There was no TV in my spot (house), so we made the sitcoms thru conversation. Within the first few months, we had a few disputes and skirmishes, but the issues with my landlord grew far more attention-worthy.

He hated the fact that I had gotten married and that another person was staying with me. I was doing some temp-work for one agency downtown on a consistent basis. They paid me weekly, so I would deposit the check immediately at the bank on 16th and Market and head back to the flat. Everything was going smooth until one week after getting paid, I did it and the check didn't register in the machine. I threw the receipt away thinking that all was good. Unfortunately, it was not.

I balanced my money from week to week to pay the rent and utilities, hook my wife up, get food, and other needs. One week would throw off the whole cycle. I told the property owner that I needed to delay paying him until I straighten out the check issue. I offered to pay him what I could and he refused. He made a big issue of the whole situation even though he knew I was good for it. A notice from the housing court came and the owner filed to evict my wife and I immediately from the property. I had paid him on time every month for a year since I was a tenant. I showed him the letter from the bank explaining the review procedure and he was not trying to hear it. He wanted me out of his house, period.

My wife was cracking up about the situation especially when the owner came to my door banging on it and threatening me with his cane. The situation was resolved in tenant's court, a week later. The agreement was I move out in thirty days and I did not have to pay him a thing.

My wife and I had some issues in that apartment sometimes leading to hollering and screaming and even further. The early-unexpected pregnancy with my first daughter, my lack of experience being in a long-term relationship, and a host of other compatibility issues started to take its toll. There were a few times that she had to stay down her mother's house to keep the peace. We would make up and she would come home. Home-girl had that street attitude. I gave that up. Somehow, we were still hanging in there for the sake of Allah. The sister stressed moving out of the apartment even before this check issue became of its location and size. Caught in the crosshairs between her fussing and the landlord, I had no choice, but to get out. I started looking in the paper and found an affordable apartment in East Oak Lane/Fern Rock Section.

Moving on to East Oak Lane, the apartment was better, roomier, and greener. The scenery was great and the neighborhood was quiet. We lived in the back and on top of the new landlord's home with a private entrance. He and his wife were straight up positive black folks. I'd have intellectual conversations with the owner and his wife from time to time. Their words were filled with wisdom and joy. My wife and I needed a breath of fresh air and this was the place I believed where we would thrive. Coming home from work, you just want to chill not be like damn, what is it now?

Big E found a job doing telemarketing out in Upper Darby at RMH Teleservices. It was a long ride from Fern Rock to Upper Darby no doubt. The money was good and the schedule gave me the daytime to chill with my peoples. At RMH, there were some good Muslim colleagues up there. One of our supervisors was Muslim and he used to always have a smile on his face. May Allah reward him and his family.

It was a long way to work, but I had no choice. The job paid salary and commission. The company would send home anyone who did not make a sale in the first two hours. My man, Kay up there was just like me. He'd be like Feeq, "I'm going to hit this campaign up today with full force." I'm chuckling saying to myself "Me too". No one wanted to get sent home especially if you lived far away. Most of us were from Philly, so was the return ride that nobody wanted to take early. The fact the salary and commission were good had moti-vated us to get that money. If not, then you'd be riding back with the lames.

Kay had brought an Islamic book discussing Islamic transactions to work one day. A few associates glimpsed over a section in the book that discussed different types of gambling. Our transactions appeared to resemble the exact examples written in the book. There was a point mentioned in the book that fire and life insurance, which we were selling over the phones, was forms of gambling. That stuck with me. If the claim was true, then I had to leave this job immediately. Religion comes first, then the paycheck. I researched the issue over a week's time and found out what was mentioned in the book was true, so I gave my resignation the following week. It was a big risk because I needed the money and did not have another job to fall back on. I rather suffer than to have my family eating from haram (unlawful) sources of income. Most of the brothers had other opinions saying "Well, we need to feed our families and there isn't anything else that I can do at the time that pays the bills". Or "This form of gambling isn't like the forms during the time of the prophet". Whatever the reason they used to justify them staying, it was not strong enough for me to stay.

My wife had begun experiencing labor pains one morning and we rushed to the hospital ASAP. Somebody's having a baby!!!!!!!!

That day was one of the most memorable days of my life from a good and bad perspective. My wife's water broke around 10:30 AM in the morning. We tried to get an ambulance, but somehow travelled on the train to Temple University hospital. The ambulance took too long. As soon as we got inside the hospital, my wife got a room instantly. We thought the baby would come out immediately, but it was an hours-long saga. I kept going out to the G for prayers and coming back immediately afterward throughout the day. Every time I came back, she had not delivered yet.

Our baby girl was born close to Maghrib (early evening). I got a full mouth blast of language during the delivery from mom to the point the doctor felt sorry for me. My face had changed in distress. She told me to just be patient. We practiced some of the Sunan (Islamic rituals) with her when she was born such as her aqeeqah (slaughtering for the child born), the removal of head hair, calling the adhan in the ear, and rubbing her teeth with dates.

A day or two later, we took our daughter home and began debating on where she should sleep. I wanted the crib and my wife wanted her in the bed with us. Supremely, the women won the battle.

Baby stuff and joy filled our apartment walls. My daughter did not cry a lot however, I did because of a toothache that just would not go away. I tried all types of pills to get rid of its pain. At night, the bad boy would return. I would be in so much pain I would try to even break it to no use. It was my first toothache ever. I ate candy and never thought that a cavity could be so painful. Somehow, the pain went away some days later and it was a relief. I continued treating myself to Dunkin Doughnuts a few times a week and as a result gained a significant amount of weight because of doing so.

———

Things began to settle down between my wife and I. No ruckus, no big issues. I was in the kitchen with the wife one day while she was cooking and discovered a letter on the ground near the door from someone writing my wife from prison. I asked her about it and she said it was an old male friend and it was not an issue. Perhaps.

As days went on, we had people come by to see my daughter. I remember we even had a class about the hadith of ten women describing their husbands in a circle. Ih was getting bigger and of course, our space was becoming restricted. Somehow, we could still have enough cash for food, clothing, and rent. My wife and family started helping me as well to foot some of the food expenses. It was a great help. Once I found a new job and settled in, the big talk of the town was Germantown Masjid.

People began moving closer to Germantown Masjid because of the arrival of Goldie. Everyone in the town wanted to get to the G for his talks. This man was known for giving knowledge-filled lectures in

English. I began listening to his tapes around 1998 when riding with some brothers back and forth to the masjid. My wife's girlfriends were calling her up on the phone saying "Sister we are moving to Germantown to get that knowledge, tell your husband that he should bring his family to come and do the same." Their husbands were insisting that we should do it too. If you read my books so far, you know that E isn't no di**rid**. I take my time and look at things closely and most of the time, people find fault in my hesitancy.

The truth was that we did not stay that far from the masjid. We were not driving at the time, but if we were, then we could have gotten up there in about 10 minutes or less. If I wanted to pray up the G from the house, I would just catch the express or local train from Fern Rock to Erie Avenue and then get on the 23 bus. It would take probably 30-40 minutes to get there. E was down for the knowledge but not down for moving close to the masjid because everybody else was doing so.

Moving up that part of Germantown was as bad as moving back to the hood regardless of whom was up there. My reason first was that I'm from Nicetown, which is almost next to that area, and even though it's not North Philly, it still was hood. Second, my wife and I were living happily and things were turning around. Yes, we needed a bigger place, but our house was in one of the best neighborhoods you could be in as an African-American and close to transport. There was no doubt the knowledge was flowing up the G, but even some of my friends advised me to stay put where I was. I felt I could just attend the lectures and go to the G like I had been doing.

The talk of moving up the G was a daily topic between my spouse and I and it became overwhelming. I gave in to my wife's wishes because she was serious about studying and getting that knowledge as well as the opportunity to get a bigger apartment for almost the same price that we were paying. We began looking for apartments in the Germantown section with the help of a few brothers. We found a real estate company around the corner from where I used to live in Mount Airy. A brother, Shaik Ali (may Allah have mercy on him), put us down with the agent and we sealed the deal. The new apartment was above the present Dawah Center location off the corner of Germantown and Manheim. It seemed perfect as my aunt lives right down the street. I could take my daughter to visit her often or so I thought.

We moved into the two-bedroom apartment on the third floor on the first of the month only a few days later. My wife and I began cleaning up the old apartment and putting things in boxes for the new apartment right away. I was happy with caution. A few weeks after we moved in, the move looked like a good decision for us because we could attend all the key lectures and reap its benefits. We discovered that we had a problem with our phone bill being so high. Someone jacked (stole) our phone card and we got charged for it. We found out that it was a sister, who got our mail before we moved in and took the phone card from it. AT&T sent the phone card to our new house before we officially moved in when we were transferring lines. After an investigation of the phone logs, we found out who was the culprit. The sister apologized and AT&T corrected the issue.

Onwards, little incidents became major disagreements between my spouse and I. One of my neighbors told me that the house had an omen. I did not pay it any mind. I am not superstitious. However, the past occupants had many issues in that apartment as I learned. My wife and I started arguing about stupid stuff like our cat eating her brush, a frakking TV, etc. Episodes intensified quickly and it got ugly. Our intent for moving into the house was for one reason; fear of Allah. The temperature was rising. The prelude for separation appeared destined; so, let us see if things would work out in the next chapter.

THE HAJJ, THE HAJJ, THE HAJJ
CHAPTER FOURTEEN

The Hajj (pilgrimage) would be a great opportunity for anyone who wanted to test his or her soul's conviction. There were a group of brothers from the East Coast who traveled to Virginia to study Arabic and some could perform Hajj with a school that they attended. They would come back to the various mosques in Philly and surrounding states; fluent in Arabic and as teachers for their communities. I was impressed. Arabic was a challenge especially for us, African-Americans, because of our deep vocal way of communication. We emphasize and stress sounds in words, often shortening them or changing their meanings.

I traveled down to the Mahad (the Arabic Language Institute in Fairfax, Virginia) to check out the school for a few days in the spring semester of

1999 and went on to study there in the fall. It was a wonderful experience meeting colleagues from all over the world trying to seek knowledge and learn Arabic. Before arriving to the institute, I had taken an Arabic class at CCP in my final semester. I studied hard and couldn't gather anything except the alphabet and few words. Our teacher was Tunisian. He was a good man who often brought sweets that his wife baked to class to give to his students. Most of my classmates knew Arabic already and were easily conversing with the instructor. Surprisingly, that they were African-Americans. Many of them came up in the Ansar movement of the late 1970s and 1980s. I befriended a brother and sister who were in the Nation of Islam during class. We struggled to grasp and found that Arabic seemed nearly impossible to grasp. We encouraged one another to study hard. At the end of the semester, I received a passing mark of C. One of them failed I believed, most likely the brother.

After my time at CCP, I decided to take an Arabic class with a brother named M at his house in North Philly. His technique of teaching was different from CCP and stretched out. I tried a few class and couldn't get anything out of them because of its unorthodox style. It was costly and the opinion was that many of his students weren't as good in Arabic even though they spent many years studying.

Both of these learning experiences and self-study helped me a bit in taking the placement exam for the Mahad in Fairfax. I reached level 2 out of 4 (Alhamdulillah). My pending off and on marital problems back in Philly were subsided. I believed that gaining that knowledge at school would help me be able to help my family religiously and perhaps increase our chemistry. That was the plan.

Somehow, I ended up getting another car from a dealer in Kensington; a Buick Skylark for only $600. It needed some work but not like the French Lemon I had before. I'd take my wife around and sometimes, she'd take it until I became firm about having the car, so I can chauffeur her around. She gave in to my demands.

I then decided to take the car to Virginia. It was a selfish move, no doubt. She was alone with my daughter and pregnant with my second. I was blind to the fact that I would be able to come home every weekend and she could use the car when I got back. My plan was to work in Virginia as well and give her my tax refund money, so she could get one for herself.

Getting around in Virginia required a whip. We had the ride although it had some issues with it, I thought it was good to go. On the highway passing through Maryland outside Baltimore on the way to the Mahad, the engine started overheating and engine light came on. After a mile or two, I stopped on the side of the road and steam was rising from the hood while the water shot out. E isn't a mechanic and knew nothing about fixing cars. I flagged down passersby in the dark and most refused. One white man pulled over, got out of his car and looked at my car. He said it was done but it could be patched up if I had a wrench. He offered me his wrench for ten dollars. I declined and asked him to push me from behind to the nearest rest stop that wasn't far from where we were. He did so for the ten dollars, I believe.

My car was left at the rest stop after unsuccessfully trying to start it up in the parking lot. I called the brothers at the house down in Virginia, al-Alhamdulillah, they came a few hours later to pick me. There are so many rest stops from Virginia to Maryland that they got lost a few times. My location was vague but somehow, they found me. When I got to Fairfax, I phoned my wife and told her about the incident. She was pissed off and had every right to be.

———

Once I got down to Fairfax and settled in, associates from the house heard my story and were astonished. They reminded me that this ordeal was no doubt, a sign of something greater to happen. There were brothers from all over the states living at Dar-as-Sunnah (the house for the out-of-state students) Our Amir (leader) of the house was a Cambodian young guy from Seattle, Washington. He'd make you smile just by looking at him. He'd been going to school for years. After school, he went straight to work at Starbucks. Some of us didn't realize that we needed to do the same until the cash started running out. Only a handful of the guys didn't work and they were fortunate.

Comfortably, into my school schedule, I went and applied for a gig at Home Depot. I was hired on the spot. It was a tough job and I always hated manual labor. E was raised in an office and that's all he ever knew. At the orientation, the staff fed us being in the Home Depot family. I wasn't into it like that and just wanted to make some ends to pay the bills. Most of the employees were buying into the theme as if they were robots programmed to punch in and out. I look at it as if it was just another gig. My work schedule was flexible. I told them that I was a student from Philadelphia and was married with children. I told them that I needed weekends off, so I could see my family. Most of the time, the weekends weren't an issue.

There were some Muslims working there with me as well. One Syrian brother used to crack me up with his prayer schedule. He would delay all his prayers to pray all of them at once at home after work including Fajr. I'm like how you doing that homie. One woman from DC was so infatuated with me that she chased me around the Home Depot at the end of our shift one night until I told her to please stop. She wanted to hug and kiss me. The girl was bodied out, with some poked-out lips and had a fat whip (car). A man's test indeed.

My man, Abd, who stayed at Dar-as-Sunnah as well, began working there shortly after me. Allah gave him an easy job, mashallah (what Allah intended). He worked in the paint department. I had a cashier job. I never was good at math. I pleaded for a change in position but they weren't going for it.

After a few months of working at Home Depot, I could bear my living expenses with ease between Philly and Virginia Alhamdulillah. No complaints from home. I tried to get back to Philly at least every two weekends. Most of the time, I kept on schedule even though I didn't have a car. I'd take the train from Fairfax to DC and then hop on the Greyhound to Philly. The commute wasn't bad at all.

In the mornings on the way to the Mahad, I'd listen to only Arabic lectures. Back at the house, we forced ourselves to speak Arabic only. As time went on, I began gradually picking up the language and benefiting from the teachers. Our subjects included Quran memorization, Grammar, Fiqh (Islamic Jurisprudence), Tafsir (explanation of the Quran), Aqeedah (creed), Adab (literature), Balagha (rhetoric), Sarf (morphology) and some others. Classes usually lasted for 4 hours and then ended at the call of prayer. We would pray at the Mahad, chat a bit afterward and then head home or go to work.

My job location (Home Depot) was down the street from the school on Hilltop Road, so I could walk there from home in about fifteen minutes. Surprisingly, I didn't expect Home Depot to intrude in one's religious affairs. I asked at least three months in advance about my wish to make Hajj (pilgrimage) making it clear that it was pending. I would need to take a leave for one month to make Hajj if the opportunity came about. My head supervisor told me just to give him a two-week notice and it shouldn't be an issue. Well, it became an issue.

I found out that our class would be making Hajj on a short notice. The school told only four days before departure after constantly telling us that it wouldn't be possible for this year's class. I still gave the head super-visor at least a two-week notice pending that I would be leaving. He straight up refused to grant it to me and told me that if I left, then I would be fired. He left me with no choices to negotiate. You already know what I was going to do, He wrote that I resigned on the pretense that I couldn't perform my duty so I couldn't get unemployment. Straight up wrong me, man! On top of this, I didn't even get my check in time for my departure, so my man Bilal, who worked at Home Depot and lived with me, gave me two hundred dollars to spend on the trip (may Allah reward him). I agreed to pay him back as soon as I got back to the states.

Right before the trip to Virginia, I discovered that my wife was pregnant with our second child. The mood swings were in full effect. You didn't bring me the right ice cream and etc. Everything had a complaint attached to it. Just deal with it, E. I wanted her to come to Hajj with me, but the school denied my request because she wasn't a student and because she was in the third trimester. I wanted her to go so badly. It could have the bond we needed. Our phone conver-sations became yelling matches. It isn't looking good, E. I kept reminding myself to be patient and her as well. My time away from home had a negative effect on her. School was only for two years and we had a vacation in the summer and on Islamic holidays beside the weekends. I reminded her of the importance of the knowledge and she'd be like OK. Being pregnant without me being present most of the time was a b****. Perhaps there were some selfish ways about me that I just couldn't rid.

Going on Hajj by myself was a blow. I didn't feel right but the opportunity was there and I had to take it. The students who were selected to go began preparing themselves for the greatest journey ever. Our papers and medical clearances had to be in order quickly. I went to a doctor somewhere in Falls Church and met him at Dar-Al-Hijrah Masjid to retrieve my immunization papers. I have some many memories of spending countless hours in that masjid studying, memorizing, buying books and tapes and meeting with other students of knowledge. Those days were so precious. Al Hamdulillah.

———

Thursday was the day of departure, so I dressed in Ihram (clothing for the pilgrimage) and headed to Dulles Airport to board the plane with 22 other pilgrims from my school and others. The itinerary was to fly to New York by private aircraft and then transfer to Saudi Airlines at JFK. The first plane was so old that you can hear the motor running inside the airplane. We were all scared to death. The Saudi Airline was on point and even had a prayer area in the back. I remember the captain of the plane even leading us for one of the prayers. Everyone was joyful and once we crossed the Miqaat (line of entry for the pilgrimage), we began to say the Talbiyah (Islam statement announcing the oneness of Allah).

We arrived in Jeddah safely some hours later. For a few hours, we had to wait for the passport control to clear us. They treated us like royalty and offered us dates and tea. Once we left the airport, we took a bus to another location and had a little trouble from some young Saudi guys trying to hitch a ride with us on our bus. For some reason, the driver lets them on at one of the checkpoints and they refused to get off until the police showed up. All of them were wearing baseball caps from the states and white thowbs (men's garments). The bus driver was startled and didn't know what to do. Many these blue-collar workers are scared of the Gulf residents out of fear that they will be deported. Our group leader intervened with the police and they got off the bus. From Jeddah, we switched planes to Madinah Al-Munawwarah. I believe. Our entourage was a group of students, parents, and professionals from DC and its suburbs. Once we landed in Madinah, it felt like we reached the most sacred ground on Earth. Everything was calm and collect.

Our hotel was right across from the Prophet's Mosque. Three-minute walking distance only, I was ready to step out to hit that mosque for 50000 prayer reward immediately. I ran into our brother and teacher, Tahir bin Wyatt (May Allah preserve him and his family) and a few others with him at the Prophet's mosque once. I was happy to see him and he was as well. Throughout the years, he advised me in private when he came home for the summer break. The city of Philadelphia particularly the Salafis looked up to the brother because he was serious about studying Islam. He was one of the first brothers up the G to study in Madinah.

We chatted a bit and then gave that Philly hug and went to go our separate ways. The Prophet's Mosque was bigger than any place I'd ever been to before. During our first night in Madinah, our teacher and reli-gious guide, Shaikh Abdul Hameed As-Saud (May Allah preserve him and his family) took us on a grand tour of the mosque after Isha prayer and while the cleaning staff was at work. Moving along, we reached the Prophet's grave and there was a second tour guide who joined us. He spoke a bit and then tried to get us to raise our hands and make prayers for the Prophet in front of the grave's doors. Our guide, Abdul Hameed stopped us from doing so. Some insisted on doing so or weren't paying attention. He mentioned that it was an innovation (bidah), but some still went on doing what they wanted.

Once we finished the tour, each person was paired up in the hotel room. The hotel was top-notch. I wish I had my own room. It was good that I didn't have to pay a thing. Alhamdulillah. The food was buffet-styled, underwear was ironed and dry-cleaned, service was VIP and the breakfast was the bomb. For the few days that we were in Madinah, I went book shopping, sight-seeing, and conversing with its inhabitants. It felt like the perfect vacation. I did notice the drivers speeding down the street like it was Need for Speed, though.

Apart from that, everything was good. The people were friendly and hospitable. As I walked through the marketplaces In Madinah, I had my first glimpses of Chanel and Gucci abayas (women's' overgarments). "Dudes must have some cake out here." I thought.

The time was now for us to hit the road to go to Mecca to perform Umrah and then Hajj. Everyone was given clear instructions on what he/she should do and if we had any questions, our group leader, Abdul Aziz Al-Saud, was there to help us.

Heading out of Madinah by air-conditioned bus to Makkah, we watched the beauty of the landscape. The heritage and the spectacle of the desert had us in awe. Not everyone was on the same page in faith, but all came with the purpose to fulfill the rites.

During one of the checkpoints, there were police officers directing the bus drivers to pull over and ordered to see the passengers' passports. The Muslims were allowed to go one way and Non-Muslims had to go another. I will never forget that moment. We continued onwards until we sighted a bridge where the overpass was designed like a Mushaf (Book of the Quran). "Wow!" I thought. "What such respect!"

Our bus arrived in Makkah in the evening. As we were climbing throughout, we shouted "Allahu Akbar" and descending, we yelled "Subhanallah". This was the moment indeed. Makkah, the birthplace of the prophet of Allah, and we are closing in on it. While climbing up the hill for a few blocks from the Haram, my colleague from the Mahad named Ram told me to look. I glanced at the wall and noticed Tupac's name written in graffiti. We couldn't stop laughing until we reached the top of the peak of the main street leading to the Haram.

The traffic was heavy even at 11:00 PM at night. It was hot outside and in the bus as we sat. Finally, after an hour or so moving sluggishly on the street leading to the Haram, we made it to the hotel. The hotel was around three blocks from the Haram. The hotel was on point and once again we were paired in couples. The room service was great and the breakfast even was better. Halal beef bacon and scrambled eggs that tasted like they were from back home. There was a mini-mall on the first floor of the hotel. If I needed to call to the states, I just buzzed the operator and they would immediately place the call.

Our group settled in quickly at the hotel and we were told to meet in the lobby to perform Umrah right away. My roommate and I prepared and headed out with the group to walk to the Haram. As I approached the Haram, I felt like I wanted to faint. This is the holiest place on Earth. The sight of the Masjid Al-Haram was mesmerizing. It surely reminded me of those 1950's black and white space movies when the aliens come to Earth and everyone is looking on as the spaceship lands. My first steps in the Haram were a heart dropper. Distant away were the troubles of life back home. "I made it" was the thought that came to mind even if it was close to 2 in the morning.

It took a few hours to finish Umrah (short pilgrimage) because of the crowd numbers. Afterward, we prayed Fajr. Imagine Fajr prayer at the Haram. Ya

Allah! This was the real deal live without the Memo-rex. Sudais lead the prayer and killed it. His voice sounded different live, but it was he no doubt. We got back to the hotel and most of us slept until almost Zuhr. After eating that slamming bacon, egg, and sausage breakfast buffet and some orange juice, I had to go out to get that 100000-prayer reward in. This was not the time to slack off. We still had a few days left before the Hajj started, so I ventured out a bit after the prayers. Our group leader and Sheikh, Abdul Hameed Al-Saud, was down with that. He scheduled our group on a tour to Masjid-Qiblatayn (the masjid where the direction for prayer changed). After offering two rakaats there, we also visited Mount Uhud and to the grounds of the battle of Badr. It was a day worth remembering.

A few days into the trip, I started looking for good places to shop around the Haram. The prices were so cheap. You could get ten black abayas for a hundred dollars. It was unbelievable. I bought some for my wife (not the ten dollar joints), a few books, a pack of kufis (head covers for the men) and some Quranic tapes and books. The shopkeepers were polite and even gave deals on the stuff.

The following day, I came into the Haram close to Zuhr time listening to Quran on my cassette player.

The guards stopped me at the entrance and told me to give them my cassette player. Really. I pleaded with them, but they said it was not allowed to bring this device into the masjid. One of them told me that I would be able to recover it once the prayer was finished on exiting the masjid. I prayed in the area closest to the door where I came in just in case they would try to get me for my cassette player.

The area where I prayed at was filled with guards and officers. Somehow, I got to pray next to them. It felt strange praying beside police officers especially coming from the states where we as African-Americans have so much trouble dealing with them. As soon as the prayer finished, I hopped up and quickly walked back to the entrance where I came in to get my cassette player back. That's when I found one of the guards listening to it. He looked like he was enjoying it. I felt a sign of relief and went back to the hotel.

Each person in our group talked about the Hajj as if it was the most difficult of pillars of Islam to perform. Our sheikh, Abdul Hameed Al-Saud checked in on us periodically to make sure that we were okay. The next morning after Fajr was something else. After the prayer and outside the masjid, one man tried to steal a purse from a woman. He thought that because it was still a bit dark outside that he would get away. Immediately, people noticed the situation after the woman started yelling and grabbed the man until the police took him away. Criminals will try you anywhere.

I tried to spend as much time as possible at the Haram. You just can't pass up that 100000 blessings (reward for every prayer performed there). Some of our group stayed in the hotel to watch TV and relax. E couldn't pass up any opportunity to get some of those limited good deeds. I watched the news and some cartoons like the Smurfs in Arabic mainly in the morning when I was waking up after Fajr in bed.

A day or two later, our group was ready to start the Hajj. Dressed in Ihram, we were told not to shave, perfume or wear closed shoes. I remember my room-mate (a brother from Kenya) and I were moving in and out of the bathroom getting ready. I paid for the ram at one of the distribution booths and was ready to head out. There was a debate among some of the group who wanted to slaughter themselves. Our sheikh advised us to keep it simple and just pay the money to the booth. From Safa to Marwah, we made our Sa-ye (7 rounds of back and forth). The place was crowded more than the Umrah when we first arrived. On Muzdilifah, we camped out until close to midnight. A hilarious instance had taken place there as we closed in on midnight.

Our group had a private gathering and camp at Muzdilifah with a notable Sheik from the Kingdom. The Sheikh was speaking to us while we ate and drank and his cell phone (the year 2000) kept ringing during the talk. He had one young man with him who knew more about the gadget then himself. It became so much of a distraction that he told his assistant to just turn it off. The assistant thought he turned it off and it rang once more. We laughed when it did. Technology can be irking at times.

After Muzdilifah, we moved onto Arafat (which I will write about shortly) and our days in Mina. Let's start with Mina. Our group met other students from the Jamiat Al-Imam sponsored Mahad (Arabic institutes) in China and Sri Lanka at a conference featuring Sheikh Fawzan (may Allah preserve him). The Chinese brothers were sharp in Arabic. I felt like a novice when I conversed with them. Anyway, before we arrived at the dawrah (conference), our delegation walked by booths of scholars giving religious instructions in Mina. I heard Sheikh Muhammad Al Munajid (may Allah preserve him) in one of those booths answering questions. Once we got inside the building where the dawrah was being held, we continued to the second floor and listened to Sheikh Fawzan give us advice on various matters.

His lecture was one to remember and the group was attentive to his words except for one brother from Pakistan who happened to be boarding with me at the hotel. Sheikh Fawzan was asked about photography and his answer was straightforward. The Saudis had been recording and videotaping the lectures of the Sheikh long before this conference. Out of spite, my roommate from Pakistan wanted to know the ruling behind videotaping these lectures. The person responsible for checking questions felt uncomfortable asking the Sheikh. He didn't want to start any commotion. When my roommate's question didn't get called on, he got upset. People tried to calm him down, but he kept ranting. The Sheikh answered the question and gave the same reply that it was not permissible. Afterward, the panel as well as the attendees were very upset at the Pakistani.

Later that evening, our group was invited on the strength of our guide (Sheikh Abdul H Al- Saud) to spend our nights at the King's personal residences right behind King Fahd's Castle at Mina. The place was so roomy and beautiful with oak doors and scenic views. In the morning, Sheikh Abdul Hameed had given us a lecture after Fajr in the guest area. He gave us some tafsir (explanation) of a few Ayats (verses) of Surah al-Tur. It was beautiful indeed. I sat as close as possible to him because I love the sheikh. He was one of our favorite teachers at the school in Virginia. He took me food shopping with him once and we had a good time. His English was good and I believe that he was in his mid-thirties at the time.

The brother, Ram that was with us from the Mahad started to experience sickness and fatigue once we got to the King Fahd's personal quarters in Mina. Something was wrong with the brother and his room-mate who also was from Chicago had some concerns that weren't normal. The Sheikh checked in and down-played it as just fatigue when the brother said he would be okay. The guards gave each one of us personal silver swipe cards to check in and out of the building. We were VIPS.

The first night at Mina before the stoning ritual, we were invited to the King's palace for a special speech close to Maghrib time. We asked our group leader, Abdul Hameed, to delay our invitation until after the Maghrib prayer, but he insisted that we meet the King at once. Loyalty matters. Once our group entered the doors of the palace, we were all astonished to see how beautiful the place was inside. A king knows how to keep his court in style. The palace guards directed us to our seats. My roommate and I sat in the same row not close to the front of where the

King was to speak. The thought of prayer keeps crossing my mind. Once a pilgrim arrives in Mina, he/she cannot combine the prayers. Knowing this, I silently stood up once the King began his talk and asked the guard closest to our row about the whereabouts of the prayer room. He pointed to the back of the palace. They say that a closed mouth will not ever get fed. There were guards and others praying back there already, so I joined. The room was full of Mushafs (Quranic books) and was simply decorated. There was nothing extravagant in its design. Your boy, E, prayed in the Musala (prayer room) of the King was the talk when I spoke about it to my colleagues after dinner. The meal was brief although the food was plenty. It appeared the King was in rush, so the guests ate fast and left quickly. Most of our group including the leader had delayed the Maghrib prayer. E knew that wasn't possible.

Once we got back to the houses in Mina that night, we discovered that our brother Ram's condition was even worse. His sickness started right before the day of Arafat. On the morning of Arafat, Ram began acting weird and wanted to remain alone in his room. His roommate complained to our guide about Ram's condition as well. He went to Arafat with us looking duped.

———

Mount Arafat was the place to be. Either before or after Arafat, our delegation had a chance to meet Sheikh Uthaymeen (may Allah have mercy on him) at a private conference. I will never forget his noble words and his way of dealing with one guy who kept taking pictures of him and the group. He ordered the guards after the third time to remove the photographer from Culver City, California's King Fahad Masjid or he claimed to be from there. I asked some years when visiting that masjid for one Jumah if there was a photographer from that mosque who attended Hajj in the year 2000. The current administration had no information on whom that person was. After that intrusion, the Sheikh went on to question our knowledge about the War of the Confederates (Ahzab). Each person kept silent and declined to answer. He chastised us for not speaking up and replying. He further stressed that we study the books of Seerah (History of the Prophet) and Tarikh (History). At the end of the dawrah (conference), the Sheikh shook everyone's hand and listened attentively to each person's conversation to him on exiting. I made dua for him and he made dua for me. Al Alhamdulillah.

Arafat is the day where you have to give it your all.

We pushed Ram to do just that throughout the day and just supplicate. At times, he got stronger and others, he was in a trance. He slowly recovered in time before Maghrib as the day of Arafat was ending. We felt happy for him.

Once the day ended, the bus came to collect us and others and we sat next to each other heading back to Mina. That's when I noticed something strange going on right behind him. There was a woman, of East African descent, rubbing the back of Ram's head. Every time I turned around, she would quickly remove her hand from his head. Once we got back to the residence, Ram became even worse. He stayed in his room until the end of Hajj. We couldn't get him out of the bed and everyone was wondering what happened to him. I mentioned the incident on the bus with Sheikh Abdul Hameed. I believed that she was working with the jinns (unseen creation) and put magic on Ram. I never saw my boy again. He was flown straight home to rejoin his parents and family after the Hajj.

After finishing the Hajj, our delegation received the pleasure of a vacation in Jeddah for about 4-5 days at a five-star hotel. The adhan at the hotel was automated which seemed so strange. People would gather in the Musalla (prayer area) waiting for the automated adhan to pray. Outside the hotel, we visited the nearby mall that had stores like Sam Goody, Baskin Robbins, and other American restaurants. The beach in Jeddah was beautiful and every woman who walked passed wore the black abaya whether they were Muslim or not. The Non-Muslim women didn't cover their hair. We prayed Jumah at one masjid in Jeddah near the sea and it was a good experience. All of us missed home, but the life in Saudi Arabia was royalty.

———

Back in America, I arrived just in time for the birth of my second child (In). The delivery was not as hectic as the first. My wife was mild-mannered this time around. Coming home wasn't as pleasant as I thought it would be. Our problems at home escalated. My absence had a lot to do with it and it was bearing down her. I wasn't expecting any drama after I finished the Hajj, but it awaited me as soon as I returned home. I got so pissed off at her that I kicked in my TV one time. With no job back in VA, life became more difficult. Hajj is a once in the lifetime opportunity. Who said that I was ever going to make it there again?

When my wife delivered the baby, there was the talk of getting divorced immediately. We just weren't compatible. Too many problems and little compromise.

Shouting, fighting, complaining, leaving the house and other issues became like wildfires that couldn't be put out permanently. Our neighbors tried to intervene to no benefit. Divorce appeared to be the most reasonable solution, except I was holding on for the sake of my girls.

The new imam at the G got a visit from my wife as things intensified. I came down the office with her and he advised me to either keep her in kindness or let her go in kindness. I was a keeper but something was pushing my wife away from me and I couldn't put my finger on the problem. I show self-restraint but a disagreement became an act of war from my counterpart. Unfortunately, being the nice guy doesn't always work out.

My determination was to get back to Virginia and complete the Arabic program no matter the outcome. As the days passed especially in the summer months, the obvious of divorcing was more prevalent. I couldn't father the thought of my kids growing up without their father being present. I had big plans for us including going outside the US to live in an Islamic country. The plan started looking like it would just be me alone.

I pondered about my girls and the reasons I didn't want them growing up in the West. My main reason was to safeguard their religion. A few days later, I received a call from the sister's wakil (guardian) for a meeting at Ridge Avenue Masjid where we had gotten married. It seemed as if it might be the end.

On the way to the masjid, my wife wanted to stop at my mother's house. It was all a ploy. My mom fell for the okeydokey, but I kept saying indirectly in front of her; let's work this thing out. What more could I do? She wanted out of the marriage. This would be a life-changing decision that would be hard to get over. My precious girls are all that I thought about.

Once we arrived down the masjid, the beans were spilled out and the cards were laid down. The Imam granted her a divorce (khula) and we left the masjid. About two weeks later, the real reason on why it didn't work out became obvious. There was no sexual healing at the end of this saga. The next book may tell you why.

ABOUT THE AUTHOR

Eric Reese was born and raised in Philadelphia, Pennsylvania and is the recipient of the first Mayoral Scholarship of Philadelphia (1993) and the Philadelphia Federation of Teachers Human Relations Award (1989).

Reach out to me at feekness@gmail.com with written testimonials and other inquiries.

Please leave a review!